Northern

**THIS IS A REVISED V1
BAKE OFF', WITH SOME NEW MATERIAL.
THE NOVELLA WAS FIRST PUBLISHED IN
2013 BY ENDEAVOUR PRESS.**

Copyright c 2021 by Susan Willis All Rights reserved. No part of this novel may be reproduced in any form by any means, electronic or mechanical (including but not limited to the Internet, photocopying, recording), or stored in a database or retrieval system, without prior written permission from the author. This includes sharing any part of the work online on any forum.

Susan Willis assets her moral right as the author of this work in accordance with the Copyright, Designs and Patent Act 1988.

        Susan Willis   www.susanwillis.co.uk

The characters, premises, and events in this book are fictitious. Names, characters, and plots are a product of the author's imagination. Any similarity to real persons, living of dead, is coincidental and not intended by the author.

CONTENTS
Chapter One – Qualifying for the Northern Bake Off
Chapter Two - Round One of the Northern Bake Off
Chapter Three – Nicola Prepares at Home
Chapter Four – Semi-Finals of the Northern Bake Off
Chapter Five – Star Baker
Chapter Six – Drinks Afterwards
Chapter Seven - The Final of the Northern Bake Off
Chapter Eight – Surprise Celebrity Judge
Chapter Nine – The Judges Decide
Chapter Ten - The Results of the Northern Bake Off
Chapter Eleven - The Winner and Loser of the Northern Bake Off

Recipes from the Final of the Northern Bake Off

Chapter One - Qualifying for the Northern Bake Off

Nicola Simpson's hands were trembling. She pushed them under her legs hoping no one would notice as she perched on a tall stool. She was sitting in a semicircle with the other nine contestants waiting for the host of the baking competition to arrive. The TV crew were busy setting up their equipment and lights around the eight benches in the kitchen.

In one hour's, time they would all take their places to start baking. Up until now Nicola hadn't felt particularly anxious but this would be the first time, they had to bake under the glare of TV lights. Now, it suddenly seemed real and quite scary.

An excited buzz ran through the room while everyone waited for the TV presenter, David Chambers to arrive. She took a deep breath and twisted a ring around her finger. Nicole had read in the programme leaflet how David had previously been a head chef in a London restaurant but now hosted most of the local television and radio food shows. Not only was he comparing the competition, but he was also the main judge, and she knew he would be the man to impress if she was to make it through to the next round.

They'd all gathered to start the competition at ten o'clock and she wished now she hadn't eaten the full English breakfast, her son, Jay had cooked. The fried bread and bacon were churning in her stomach. She looked at the man sitting on the next stool and licked her dry lips.

He smiled reassuringly. He'd introduced himself earlier as Simon Jones. A forty-nine-year-old widower and self-taught baking addict. He sat with his long legs in brown corduroy trousers spread wide on the stool with his hands calmly resting in his lap.

He looks laid back, she thought and felt beads of sweat form on her top lip. Nicola remembered the fantastic Yorkshire curd he'd made in the qualifying round and knew out of everyone he would certainly make it through to the next round.

He smiled. 'It's a bit different to last week when we cooked on our own and handed in our finished bakes,' he said. 'It's going to be nerve-wracking cooking under these lights and knowing everyone in the North East will be watching us.'

She gulped and tapped her foot repeatedly on the stool leg. Maybe he wasn't as cool as he looked and was one of those people who could easily hide their feelings. Nicola knew she was the total opposite. 'I know, my hands are shaking already,' she said rubbing her sweaty palms down her trousers. 'And when David Chambers arrives to watch us and make comments, I'll be even worse!'

He put his hand on her arm and gave it a gentle squeeze. 'You'll be fine once you start baking,' he said. 'I think it's best to get your mind on your recipe straight away and concentrate on what you're doing. I'm going to try and ignore the lights and everything else that is going on around me.'

'Oh, right,' she mumbled. 'Thanks for the tip.'

With the noise of the door opening, she jerked her head back to the front of the room and heard the TV crew start to clap as David swaggered into the room.

Nicola had watched him on TV programmes and thought him a handsome and charismatic guy, but nothing could have prepared her for his appearance in person. He was, she decided, drop-dead gorgeous. At forty-one he was tall and slim with broad shoulders. His fair hair was thinning slightly but this did nothing to hinder his smooth-skinned face and sparkly blue eyes. Nicola's knees felt weak and her insides did a treble somersault.

'Good morning, everyone,' he said in a loud voice. He held his hands loosely behind his back as he strode towards the long serving table at the front of the room. 'Welcome to our first, and hopefully not our last, Northern Bake Off, here is sunny Newcastle.'

Two chairs had been strategically placed in front of the table and he ran a self-assured hand along the back of a chair while everyone smiled at each other in anticipation. A young guy hurried to David with a microphone which he easily clipped around his ear and adjusted the mouthpiece. 'I'm just going to run through some details before we record the episode and start the competition.'

She glanced at Simon who was obviously hanging upon every word David spoke and forced herself to concentrate.

Dressed in slim-fitting black jeans and a grey shirt, David began to step lightly around the table while he spoke. 'I was amazed at the standard of entries into the competition and didn't know we had so many skilled and proficient bakers living here. So, I think,' he said grinning along the line of ten contestants.

'You should all start by giving yourselves a round of applause for getting to the final places.'

Everyone looked at each other and began to clap and smile. Her shoulders relaxed a little and Simon nodded at her.

David left the table and walked towards them. 'When I came last week to judge your bakes, I distinctly remember a fantastic three-layered berry sponge which was so light it was simply delicious. So, who made that?'

Nicola's heart soared with happiness and pride when she realised he was talking about her sponge. Tentatively she raised her hand. 'I…I did,' she croaked. Simon grinned at her and the group began to clap again.

'Fabulous,' he said and stood in front of her with the camera at his side. His blue eyes danced as he stared at her. 'Well, I couldn't have done better myself,' he said. 'And you are?'

She could see her face in the lens of the camera and shuffled on her stool. Frantically, she wracked her brain trying to remember her own name. Her mouth was dry, but she moistened her lips and managed to whisper, 'My name is Nicola.'

With a smile playing around his mouth, he looked her up and down. 'And is Nicola a cook?'

'Oh, no,' she gasped. 'I'm a librarian but I only work three days a week now.'

She looked into his eyes. Her throat thickened and her cheeks flushed. She couldn't believe such a devastatingly attractive man was giving her his undivided attention.

'There now,' he said loudly and strutted back towards the table. 'Isn't this what the competition is all about? Here we have a librarian who can bake a sponge with the same expertise as a professional cook – it's amazing!'

Nicola took a deep breath of relief when the camera was wheeled away from her and the director stopped filming.

David explained the cameras and lights to everyone and how he would walk around the room while they were baking to chat about their cooking experience and the reasons for entering the competition. He told them to remain as calm and natural as they could and stressed that they were not to worry about mishaps, spillages or disasters. The director would edit the sessions and what wasn't needed would end up on the cutting room floor.

'Okay,' he shouted enthusiastically. 'Are we all ready?'

Nodding and answering in agreement they all stood up and hurried to their benches. Nicola was pleased to see Simon edge his way to the bench next to hers in the middle section of the room and she smiled. It felt good to see his friendly face near her.

The lights shone brightly, and the camera was placed once more in front of David while the director called, 'And action.'

David smiled into the lens and began his introductory speech thanking Northumbria University for the use of the facilities and describing the next three weeks of programs. Nicola stared at him completely entranced. He was easily the most exciting man she'd ever met.

When she'd dressed in the morning, she hadn't given a second thought to her choice of clothes and had pulled on well-worn jeans and a black T-shirt. Now as she tied a long white apron around her waist, she felt shabby and drab.

Why, oh why, she cursed, hadn't she found time to style her brown curls and pay more attention to her make-up. She'd read somewhere that the lens of a camera could age people and she prayed it wouldn't make her look older than her thirty-nine years. It might make the few wrinkles around her eyes stand out more and remembered how her mam had always called them laughter lines. Even as a child Nicola had been known for her bubbly personality.

She fiddled with the utensils on the bench and decided that although it was too late now to change her appearance she would smile as much as possible to make the best of the situation.

David explained to the viewers. 'In my opinion, England is the home of honest baking and we beat the rest of the world when it comes to simple great bakes which offer pure pleasure. Who needs the hassle of French crêpes, or American whoopie pie, when you can enjoy a seriously sticky Chelsea bun or a homemade fruit cake?'

'And cut,' the director shouted.

His raised voice made Nicola jumped back to reality. The crew came around the benches and showed everyone where the gaffer-taped spots were on the floor. They explained how they were to stand in the exact place if David was being filmed while talking to them.

Simon leaned across to her and whispered, 'By the way, your sponge last week was fantastic and well worth his praise. Where did you learn to bake like that - surely not from reading cookbooks in the library?'

'No, of course, not,' she said and giggled. 'My mam taught me to bake when I was little and although I've never had a daughter, I have taught my son to cook. He's just started at Durham University and is the only one in his digs who can make a meal.'

Simon smiled and nodded. 'Ah, well he'll certainly be popular with his flatmates.'

While the director and crew were deep in discussion David wandered across to the two front benches and Nicola thought he was making a beeline for her again. She sighed in disappointment when he stopped in front of a young girl, called Gemma.

Nicola could hear their conversation and instantly felt her stomach harden. She knew what it was like to have his attention and didn't want anyone else to benefit from his one-to-one conversation. Which, she chided herself, was quite ridiculous.

Simon whispered, 'He certainly knows how to charm everyone, doesn't he?'

Nicola smiled. 'Oh, yeah, he's lovely,' she mumbled to herself then stared at the back of Gemma's pretty head.

Gemma looked about twenty-five. She was tall, very slim, and probably a size ten, Nicola thought and clicked her tongue. Gemma wore her long blonde hair in a single plait down her back. Her baby-blue eyes were sultry, and her complexion was flawless.

Hmm, Nicola mused, she was the same age as the girl her husband had run off with two years ago. She had been his new PA and from day one he'd been besotted with her. What was it with middle-aged men, she thought? Did they reach their forties and decide they had to work backwards in age?

It was a question she'd thrown at her husband before he headed out of the door. His response had been to sadly shake his head and tell her it hadn't been intentional. He had simply fallen in love. And what about our love, she'd wanted to scream at him. And the love for your son? But she'd lifted her chin and let him leave without more altercation.

She listened now as Gemma told David. 'Well, I teach food technology in a secondary school.'

Nicola could see David staring longingly at Gemma's full breasts peeking out of her tight-fitting shirt.

Really, Nicola groaned, was there any need to open all three top buttons. She glanced down at her own small chest hidden in the T-shirt and knew she couldn't compete with Gemma. But perhaps she could win him over with her sparkling personality and fabulous baking, she thought and looked around the large room.

The room was warm with all the ovens turned on, and the overhead strip lighting alongside the TV lights was dazzling. However, it was spotlessly clean, and their workstations were equipped with a good-sized food mixer and a square gas hob. Two big fridges and freezers stood against the longest wall and various pieces of catering equipment were placed around the room.

She watched Simon looking in cupboards and drawers under his bench to assess what implements they had to work with and was impressed at his forethought.

'That's a good idea,' she said. 'I suppose we should familiarise ourselves with what equipment we've got to do the challenge. I do hope it's something I've baked before, don't you?'

While he knelt in front of an open cupboard, he looked up at her. 'Hmm, it would be an advantage, but I only know the recipes that I can bake which were the ones my late wife taught me. So, if it's an obscure French recipe I'll be lost!'

She frowned. 'But surely it won't be as complicated as the recipes on the BBC programme?' She bit her bottom lip. 'I mean, it is just a local competition.'

He stood up, straightening his trousers, and tucked the cream checked shirt into the waistband. 'Well, from what David was saying earlier he seems to think we're all such great bakers he might give us a tougher challenge.'

'Oh, dear,' she muttered and rubbed the back of her neck. She was beginning to wish she hadn't listened to her friend, Susan's encouragement to enter the competition and had stayed at home. But, she brightened, then she wouldn't have met David and stared at him across the room.

The director shouted about sound issues and told them all to go back into the hospitality room for a coffee. She filed out of the room behind Gemma and Simon.

***

12

The small hospitality room adjacent to the kitchens had three comfortable sofas and a coffee vending machine. She sat down towards the end of a sofa and Gemma settled beside her while Simon went to the machine to get coffee.

They were sitting in front of the only window in the room and Nicola gazed out at the car park to avoid looking at Gemma.

'I just wanted to say,' Gemma said. 'How marvellous your berry sponge looked last week, is it a recipe of your own?'

Nicola was surprised at the compliment and smiled. She lifted her chin. 'It was a basic recipe from my mam's cookbook but then I added my own signature to it.'

Other than the fact that David had singled Gemma out for his friendly chat, she had no other reason to dislike the girl. She tensed her shoulders. There was something behind Gemma's sickly-sweet personality that made her wary. Something that didn't quite add up.

Simon arrived back with coffee and sat down next to Gemma grinning like a teenager.

Jeez, Nicola thought, it was as if the girl were a mouth-watering cupcake that they all couldn't resist.

Gemma trailed her long plait over her shoulder and stroked it while she smiled at Simon thanking him for the coffee.

He said, 'I hope you don't mind me asking, but do you have any Scandinavian blood in your family because you certainly look more Swedish than English.'

'Oh, nooo,' she tittered. 'I'm from Leeds and have just moved up here to Newcastle. I'm renting a flat in Jesmond and luckily I got the teaching job I've always wanted.'

Simon nodded. 'Ah, so you're living near to Nicola, she lives in Gosforth,' he said. 'And what does your boyfriend think of you entering the competition. I bet he can't wait to see you on TV?'

Nicola sipped the hot coffee and leaned forward to hear her answer. Gemma was bound to have a trendy young guy hanging around.

Gemma smiled. 'Well, I don't have a boyfriend yet. But I was hoping if I joined in some activities in the area, I'd make new friends. It's true what they say about everyone in the North being very friendly.'

Simon raised a dark eyebrow. 'I can't believe a lovely young girl like you doesn't have a boyfriend. I thought you'd be beating the guys off with a whisk,' he said and chortled. 'Excuse the pun!'

All three were laughing at his joke and drinking their coffee when David arrived then perched on the end of the sofa next to Nicola. An air of excitement simmered between the three of them that David had chosen their group to sit with.

'Bunch up, Nicola,' David said.

She shuffled along the sofa and David sat next to her. He draped his arm along the back of the sofa close to her shoulders. She could smell his Paco Rabanne aftershave and glowed with pleasure as his leg rested next to hers. Her own legs were hot and sweaty in her jeans as the thick denim stuck to the plastic sofa. She wished that she had worn a skirt and could have enjoyed David's closeness in comfort.

David ran a hand through his floppy, blonde hair. 'We often have times like this with technicalities going awry and sometimes it can take hours to get it all sorted,' he said. 'There's often days when I'm at work up to fourteen hours a day!'

'Hmm, that's tough,' Simon said then frowned. 'I'm an accountant and thankfully a steady nine to five type of guy.'

Nicola tried to join in the conversation, but her mind was whirling. She couldn't seem to think in a rational frame of mind when David was near her and felt like a tongue-tied adolescent.

David asked Simon where he was from and he told them he lived in a small country cottage on the outskirts of Hexham. And how his wife had died of breast cancer three years ago.

Nicola looked at Simon's sad eyes while he talked about his late wife and leaned across to give his arm a gentle squeeze.

She couldn't imagine how she would have coped if her husband had died. However there had been times shortly after her husband left when Jay had cried for his dad in his bedroom. It had torn at her heart like a physical pain and she'd wished his father had died and wasn't shacked up with a young girl. But now that she had moved on with her life, she wouldn't wish death on anyone.

'God, that's crap,' David said quietly. 'I thought I had it bad when my wife ran off to live with a professor who's sixty-five with a long grey beard!'

Nicola gasped. She was stunned at this admission. How on earth could a woman with an iota of sense leave a lovely guy like this for an old man. She longed to know more but wasn't sure how to do this without sounding nosey.

However, Gemma was one step ahead and gently shook her head. 'I think she must have been crazy, David.'

David focussed a grateful smile on Gemma. 'That's exactly what I thought,' he said and shrugged his shoulders. 'But it was over a year ago now and she tells me she's never been happier.'

Nicola glared at Gemma's amiable face. This girl was beginning to get under her skin now. She seemed to be hogging Simons and David's attention.

Not wanting to be left out, she turned to David and said, 'It was Simon who made the amazing Yorkshire curd tart last week, can you remember it?'

David glanced at her then nodded. 'Wow! Yes, of course, that was my second choice after your berry sponge,' David said. He turned his attention back to Simon. 'It was amazing – where did you get the recipe from?'

Just as they began to talk about finding recipes the director put his head around the door and called them back to start again.

Chapter Two - Round One of the Northern Bake Off

While David looked into the camera and began his introductory talk again Nicola recalled the last few weeks. It was Susan who had spotted the advert for the competition.

'But you've got to enter - you're the best cook I've ever known!' Susan had cried then giggled. 'And I'll willingly be a guinea pig to taste your recipes.'

Nicola had been uncertain. 'Well, I know I'm a good baker,' she'd said. 'But am I up to the standard for the competition? I mean, are they looking for an advanced level because I'm more of a home cook.'

But Susan had persisted, and every time Jay rang, he badgered her, until eventually she'd filled in the entry form. She also knew that Jay worried about her being alone in their big family home since he'd left for university which was the last thing she wanted.

She wanted him to enjoy his time and be carefree as a young student should be. Of course, she'd heard about the empty-nest scenario and although she had missed him, she'd built up her social life by joining a reading group and local swimming classes. At the time, she had thought this competition was another form of interest and recreation but hadn't anticipated the level of stress associated with it all.

Her entry bake had been a chocolate and orange Northumberland twist which she'd made many times before. It had always been a big hit with friends and family therefore she hadn't been totally surprised when she was accepted.

She sneaked a look at Simon who smiled and gave her a thumbs up signal. She swallowed hard knowing that although she was still glowing with the success of her berry sponge, the technical challenge was scary. Would she be out of her depth and have to leave the competition in total embarrassment because she wasn't good enough.

David finished speaking and she shook herself to concentrate.

'And now, bakers,' David said. 'For this technical challenge we are going to ask you to make a strawberry millefeuille. And for the viewers at home this is like a posh custard slice.'

He walked towards the two ladies standing at the front benches and picked up a punnet of strawberries from their trays. 'And,' he said. 'Because this is summertime, I've brought along some of our great English strawberries.'

Joy of joys, Nicola thought and grinned. This was something she had made before and her pastry was usually a success. She glanced across at Simon who nodded which she hoped meant that he too, was at ease with the choice of recipe.

'This technical bake challenge separates the wheat from the chaff,' David continued then laughed at his own joke. 'With one basic recipe, and the same ingredients and instructions, we are asking our bakers to produce the finished millefeuille in any variation. And because this group of eight people are seriously good bakers and the standard is already so high, to make the challenge more interesting, I'm going to ask them to create their own decoration. It will be a test of their technical knowledge and experience. So, you bakers will be laid bare in this task and the pressure is really on!'

Nicola took a big sigh of relief that the millefeuille challenge was something she classed as an easy recipe to follow. She stood with her arms folded in eagerness to get started.

The crew hurried around everyone sliding recipe sheets onto their benches, while David continued, 'Well, bakers, you have the recipe sheets in front of you now. And I just want to give the viewers the definition of this recipe from, The Larousse Gastronomique. It is a small pastry of French origin known as the Napoleon and dates to the 19th century. It consists of thin layers of puff pastry separated by layers of cream, which may be flavoured with jam or some other filling. The top is covered with icing sugar, fondant icing or royal icing.'

All the contestants nodded as he spoke, and David began to walk around them with the camera following him.

Nicola noticed when he passed Gemma's bench, she had looked into the camera cocking her pretty head to one side and asked, 'So, we need to follow your recipe with the pastry, custard and the strawberries we've been given but can put it together as we see fit?'

'Exactly!' David said. 'With all the store cupboard ingredients available I want to see how you can create a different appearance. It's up to you what and how many layers you decide upon and how you arrange the millefeuille.'

Gemma smiled fully into the camera lens and nodded her head in understanding.

Nicola sighed with irritation. So, she was a good actress on top of everything else, she mused. Well, let's just see how good a baker she really is and how she copes with puff pastry on a hot day.

David continued, 'The actual recipe should take around two hours but I'm going to be lenient and give you an extra fifteen minutes to concentrate on your decoration. So, if I were you guys, I'd get straight on with my pastry and use the time while it's resting in the fridge to think about the fantastic millefeuille you can create,' he said.

He gave the viewers a dazzling smile which showed off his perfect white teeth then shouted, 'YOU HAVE TWO HOURS AND FIFTEEN MINUTES – NOW BAKE!'

The director shouted cut and Nicola saw David relax his shoulders. He sat down at the table as the director strode across to him and they bent their heads in whispered discussion.

Nicola knew the decoration she was going to attempt because she'd seen similar in a magazine and had tried the arrangement on another dessert. Instead of numerous layers with jam and custard which could look fussy, her decoration would only have two thick, clean layers. One with whole glazed small strawberries and the other with a compact layer of vanilla custard.

And, she thought striding towards the ingredients in the fridge, if there was a fresh lime, her plan would work. She discovered a lime and grinned then gathered her ingredients and set to work. Simon had been right, she thought. Once her mind was engrossed in doing what she loved, her confidence soared, and the nervous stress soon disappeared. David's instructions for making the puff pastry were similar to the way she'd made it in the past and she began to weigh out the white flour, salt, butter and cold water.

The camera was rolling again, and David walked to the back of the room where a large man called, Thomas with thick-rimmed glasses was chatting to him while he weighed out his ingredients.

'Hi, Thomas, it's not the best temperature in this room to make puff pastry but as with many summer desserts they often prove troublesome on a hot day,' David said laughing. 'And as we don't often get sunny days like this here in Newcastle, the best advice I can give to bakers is to keep everything, especially your hands, as cool as possible.'

Thomas grunted at David. 'I'm sweltered already,' he complained. He wiped his red forehead with a piece of kitchen roll and then held his fat fingers up towards the camera. 'I've got big butcher's hands so this could turn out to be a real mess!'

David roared with laughter and continued chatting to him while Nicola ignored the rest of their conversation and smoothed her butter into a soft pat.

He was right, she thought. The room was very hot because it only took minutes to soften the hard yellow butter as she began to roll out the pastry into a large rectangle. With the sun beating through the large window next to her bench she worked quickly. Gently, she floured the pastry and placed the butter in the centre then folded the three edges of the pastry around to form an envelope shape. Turning the dough swiftly to her left she began to roll again and fold once more. She covered the dough with clingfilm and placed it in the fridge for the first twenty-minute rest and saw Simon doing the same. He gave her a friendly wave and she smiled back at him giving him a thumbs up.

Nicola glanced towards the front two benches where she noticed the contestants struggling with the rolling technique David had written on the technical sheet. He stood watching them intently as one lady got herself into such a fluster, she confessed that she couldn't remember which was her left and right hand.

Nicola could also see how the other lady's butter was too near the edge and would probably ooze out, which had happened to her in the past. But, she decided, that's what baking was all about. You have to make your own mistakes and try again until you get it right. She sighed; it was just a pity that it was happening to them here in the competition. Feeling sorry for them but knowing it wasn't allowed, she fought the urge to go to their aid.

While waiting for twenty minutes she began to weigh out her ingredients for the vanilla custard. She knew the gelatine stage would be crucial because it had to be thick enough to hold its shape in the layer between the pastry rectangles. While she brought milk, cream, and vanilla to the boil in a saucepan David stopped with the camera in front of Simon.

'You seem comfortable with the puff pastry, Simon?' David asked.

Simon flushed bright red in the face as he shuffled his feet onto the gaffer tape while the camera did a close-up shot. 'W…well, I have made it a few times at home but mainly to make savoury recipes,' he said fiddling with his watch. 'But this will be the first time I've made a dessert with it.'

David nodded. 'Great. I'm sure you'll do a fine job. Now, I'll just let the viewers know the reasoning behind resting the dough for twenty minutes in the fridge,' he said leaving Simon and walking over to the fridge. 'It's necessary to keep the dough cool which gives the gluten strands in the flour time to relax. It stops the dough from becoming stretchy, which makes it harder to roll and can also make the pastry tough.'

Nicola nodded in silent agreement and then smiled reassuringly across at Simon whose colour had returned to normal. He grinned back and began to mix his custard.

With her custard mix finished and set to cool, the timer buzzed, and she removed her pastry, repeated the rolling and folding regime another twice then re-covered it once more and placed it back in the fridge. She noticed Simon look at her with disbelief. He mouthed the words, thank you, and Nicola realised he'd forgotten to set his timer for twenty minutes.

During this rest period she made a sugar glaze for the strawberries and a sorbet by passing the largest strawberries through a sieve to purée. She mixed them with lime juice, water and caster sugar then churned the mix in an ice cream maker.

She felt well into her stride now and was thoroughly enjoying herself as the timer bleeped again and she repeated the rolling regime. This time, however, she rolled the pastry into a large rectangle, placed it onto a baking tray, covered it with clingfilm and followed the instructions for a final rest of thirty minutes.

Choosing the smallest strawberries in her punnet she removed the stalks and made sure they looked perfect in shape and size. She inhaled the damp warmth of the strawberries and sighed with pleasure. If ever there was a smell of summer, then this was it.

With five whole caramelised almonds toasting in the oven and her piping bag ready for the custard she felt well ahead of herself in timing.

She wandered across to Simon. 'I seem to have finished quicker than everyone else which is worrying. Maybe I've forgotten something really important?'

'No, I don't think so, Nicola. I've been watching and you're just very well organised and methodical in everything you do,' he said. He grinned at her while wrapping his pastry on the baking tray with film.

They chatted quietly about the other contestants and Simon commented that Gemma looked just like a teacher. Totally cool and unflappable.

Hmph, Nicola snorted under her breath as she headed back to rescue her pastry from the fridge. Before she put the baking tray into the oven, she placed another tray over the top to keep the pastry flat. David had given the oven temperatures to use but not the allocated time but knowing from experience she set the timer for twelve minutes.

Just as she removed her perfect golden-brown pastry from the oven and set it aside to cool, she jumped to see David standing in front of her.

He boomed, 'BAKERS, YOU'VE GOT ONE HOUR LEFT.'

Nicola noticed the camera had been led away by one of the crew while he stood in front of her bench and purposely stared into her eyes.

She relaxed her shoulders and matched his gaze then smiled at the sight of his sparkling blue eyes. In a certain light they were nearly turquoise, and she wondered if he wore tinted contact lenses. She mused, Richard Gere, eat your heart out, and gave him her best smile.

He placed well-manicured fingers over the top of her hand. 'I knew you'd be giving me something very special, Ms Librarian,' he said and almost purred. 'I can tell I'm going to have to keep my eye on you.'

She giggled and twirled a curl of her hair around her finger. 'Well, I've made a little extra to go with mine. After all, you did say you wanted us to be creative?'

He was flirting with her and she loved it. There was something distinctive in the way he looked at her, certainly more than any of the other women, except for Gemma, of course. But, she decided, the girl was far too young for him.

He leaned forward over the bench and whispered in her ear. 'And is there a Mr Simpson waiting for you at home?'

Her heart was racing. She inhaled the clean manly smell from him and could feel her legs weaken as the desire to touch him flew through her body at great speed. It was years since she'd felt such strong attraction and she swallowed hard. 'Oh, no,' she whispered. 'My husband left a few years ago. I've been divorced for a while now.'

'Hmmm, very interesting,' he said in a louder voice and walked away from her.

Comments of dismay and frustration were coming from all over the room as the contestants removed their pastry sheets from the oven.

Nicola heard snippets from the two ladies at the front. 'I'm not sure what I'm doing.' and then, 'But if I do that it'll crack!'

She heard Thomas groan loudly and state that his first encounter with puff pastry had been an absolute disaster.

The cameras were set to roll again, and David called out, 'BAKERS, YOU HAVE FIFTEEN MINUTES TO DECORATE.'

Nicola found a rectangular white serving plate for her millefeuille and began to build up the finished dessert. If the strawberry sorbet worked as she hoped, it would look sensational. Carefully she placed the base piece of pastry down towards the end of the plate.

Gently, she stood her layer of small whole strawberries, one by one, onto the pastry with their ends uppermost. She piped custard onto another pastry piece and gently sandwiched another pastry piece on top. Whispering a little prayer to herself she placed the sandwich onto the top of the strawberries.

She took a deep gratifying sigh as the layers and strawberries were stable enough to stand firm, and then lightly scattered icing sugar on the top. Finally, she placed three caramelised whole almonds with the nibs all pointing downwards in a row onto the pastry and stood back wiping her hands on a tea towel.

To complete her plate decoration, she scooped an egg-shaped dollop of smooth strawberry sorbet and placed it on the opposite end of the plate and wiped it clean from scattered icing sugar.

David now shouted, 'TIME IS UP, BAKERS! STEP AWAY FROM YOUR MILLEFEUILLE.'

When her name was called, she walked slowly with trembling legs and carried the dessert to the front table. Carefully, she placed the plate behind her photograph which was facing into the room and away from David who would do the blind tasting.

Simon came to join her, and they stood like frightened school children waiting and looking at the other millefeuilles being taken to the table. The crew arranged their stools in a line in front of the table and they all took their places.

Unable to see which dessert belonged to which contestant David started at one end and worked his way through them all tasting as he went and making comments.

Gemma's was first and he commented upon the intricate four layers of pastry, custard and strawberry preserve which were traditionally well done. After swallowing a mouthful, he proclaimed the texture and flaky taste of the pastry was excellent. Nicola looked along the row at Gemma and saw her lift her shoulders and smile ever so sweetly into the camera.

The next two desserts from the ladies at the front were not up to the standard required to go further in the competition because the pastry texture was too tough and chewy. David told them that it was obvious they hadn't followed his regime of resting time in the fridge.

Thomas's millefeuille collapsed in the centre while David examined it, but he did comment that it had one of the better flavour profiles. And then after shaking his head he moved swiftly onto Simon's dessert.

'This is a very good effort, and my only criticism is that the custard is a little thin and as you can see everyone,' he said and pointed in a close-up shot. 'It is starting to ooze out of the layers. You just need a little more gelatine next time.'

Nicola held her breath and closed her eyes for a few seconds while David looked at her serving plate then grinned into the lens of the camera. He'd deliberately left hers until last and she prayed it wasn't because there was something wrong with it.

He stood back from the table and folded his arms. 'At the beginning of this challenge, I asked the contestants to be creative and show me something different. And out of all the eight desserts this is the only baker who has tried to give the millefeuille a unique appearance. It looks absolutely fabulous! The simple two layers of whole strawberries and vanilla custard with almonds on top gives it a clean uncluttered appearance, and the serving of sorbet on the side looks exquisite.'

He leaned forward, inhaled deeply then took a fork and broke into the dessert. He sighed and rolled it around his mouth then gasped. 'The strawberry aroma from the sorbet is delightful. The pastry is a perfect crisp flake with a delicious light taste, and the custard has just the correct amount of vanilla flavouring,' he said then popped a whole strawberry and almond into his mouth. 'Oh, God, the combination of all three together is simply divine.'

Everyone in the group looked at her and she could feel her face blushing. Her heart soared and she nipped the side of her leg to make sure she wasn't dreaming. She couldn't believe what he'd just said and murmured her thanks. Simon squeezed her arm and mouthed the word, congratulations.

David grinned into the camera. 'I can now place the millefeuille in order,' he said.

Explaining who was last, he worked his way up to the top three. Simon came third, while Gemma was a close second.

'However,' he said and waved his arm flamboyantly around them all. 'Without a shadow of doubt our *star baker* from this round is, Nicola Simpson.'

Everyone clapped and congratulated her then gathered around as she sat on the stool beaming. Simon put his arm along her shoulder and gave it a quick squeeze but then stood back as David approached.

'That millefeuille is sensational,' he said. 'And I can honestly say it would grace any top-class French patisserie. Well done and congratulations!'

Chapter Three – Nicola Prepares at Home

Nicola's head was spinning with everything that had happened as she drove home to Gosforth and pulled up outside their large terrace house. She grinned like a fool at her elderly and grumpy next-door neighbour then flew through the hall on an all-time high. Every time she thought about winning round one and how well her strawberry millefeuille had been received she tingled and wanted to giggle. To be pronounced star baker in the first part of the competition was more than she could have dreamt about. She punched the air and shouted, 'YES' at the top of her voice.

Remembering how David had placed one of his hands over hers she felt her cheeks flush then hurried up the stairs and into the bathroom. She stripped off her jeans and T-shirt then stood in front of the full-length mirror. In her black lace bra and size fourteen panties, she groaned out loud. Spinning around she looked at what she thought of as her humongous bottom. She hated it with a vengeance.

It was the one part of her body that always made her miserable. But, she reasoned, could it really be that bad if David were flirting and coming on to her. He must have been looking at her bottom all day in the jeans and had still been interested enough to ask if she was married. So, maybe he was like her ex-husband and really did like big-bottomed girls?

Whooping and giggling she stood under the shower roaming her hands over her body in the soapy shower gel and hot water. God, it felt like forever since she had been so turned on and excited by a man. And what a man he was. He was funny and cute and suave all at the same time. When he had touched her skin, she'd felt goosebumps all over.

***

'And the greatest thing about it all,' she said to her friend, Susan. 'Is that I get to do it all again next week!'

They were sitting at her kitchen table drinking wine while Nicola told her all about round one. 'So, along with myself, Simon, Gemma, Thomas, and another older lady, we have all gone through to the semi-finals!'

Her description of Gemma made Susan laugh until her double chin wobbled. 'Oh, Nicola, I'm so pleased you've enjoyed the experience. I've been feeling a little guilty thinking of how I'd badgered you into entering the competition,' she said. 'But now I'm sure you are going to win!'

Nicola took a deep breath and looked at Susan's big grey eyes. It was just like her to fret over something like this. Susan was probably the kindest person she'd ever met, and they'd been great friends since schooldays. 'Hey, you didn't badger me but gave me the kick up the jacksy that I needed,' she said.

Susan squeezed her hand. 'Go, on, tell me more?'

Nicola smiled. 'Well, Gemma's millefeuille came a very close second to mine, so she is definitely the one I have to beat,' she said. 'In more ways than one because David seems to like her too,' she said then grimaced.

Susan nodded and pursed her lips. 'Hmph, the little upstart!'

Nicola went on to describe David and how he'd made her feel.

'Well, I like him already,' Susan said and grinned. 'If he can put a buzz in your step like this then he must be okay, and it'll be so exciting to see you on TV. I can't remember the last time I saw you look so happy!'

'I know,' Nicola giggled. 'But next week I must look my best. I'm going to have something done with this unruly mop I call my hair,' she said. 'And I might pop into the beauty salon to see if they can do something clever with make-up to hide the size of my big nose.'

Susan tutted and shook her head sharply. 'Now you're just being silly. There's nothing wrong with your nose and once he looks into those big brown eyes of yours and you give him a big smile he'll be won over in seconds,' she said. 'He won't be able to resist you!'

Nicola sipped her wine. 'Ah, you're bound to say that,' she said leaning across to stroke Susan's arm. 'You're my friend and always see the best of me, but others are not so kind. And when I think of myself up against the likes of young Gemma, well, I'll have to do something?'

Avoiding Susan's eye, she looked at her new shiny red kitchen cabinets. She'd had the kitchen revamped last year and had been fond of the saying, out with the old and in with the new. It had been part of her resolve to push all her memories into the past where they belonged. However, as she looked around now all she could recall was the pain and hurt when she'd first seen a photograph of her ex-husband with his young partner. Jay had the photograph in a frame on his bedside table and it still made her seethe.

She felt her mood deflate. Who was she trying to kid, there was no way she could compete against a twenty-four-year-old?

Susan poured more wine into Nicola's glass. 'Sweetheart, we've been through this so many times. You have to let it go,' she soothed.

'I know, Susan, but it's so hard starting again when you've been dumped for a girl nearly half your age. If only she'd been a woman of my own age it wouldn't have hurt so much.'

She looked at Susan remembering when he'd first left and how she'd sat crying on her friend's shoulder with her big arms holding her tight. Susan's support had been something she would never forget.

'He was a complete tosspot,' Susan stated firmly. 'Any decent man wouldn't even look at girls that age, let alone fancy one!'

Susan lifted Nicola's chin and cocked her head to one side. 'Come on, if you let those memories spoil the rest of your life then he's won, hasn't he?'

Susan was right, she decided. All she needed was to rebuild her confidence. She pulled her shoulders back and smiled. 'Okay, so I can't beat Gemma with my age and looks but I know I can beat her with my baking skills,' she said. 'And the proof, my friend, will be in the pudding!'

Susan clapped her hands together and laughed.

Nicola grinned at her own pun. 'You're so right, Susan. All I need is to experiment again with a new man and who better to practise with than David Chambers!'

Chapter Four – Semi-Finals of the Northern Bake Off

On the morning of the semi-finals Nicola could hardly contain herself with excitement. She'd treat herself to a spray tan two days earlier and had her mop of curls straightened into a long sleek bob.

Jay had arrived home on a fleeting overnight visit and had proclaimed that he hardly recognised her. 'Oh, Mam, you're bound to win with your chocolate torte. It's the best,' he raved. 'I've told all my mates that you're the greatest cook and we can't wait to watch you on TV!'

'Let's see what happens,' she cautioned. 'There are some incredibly good bakers in the competition and it's not easy baking under the glare of the camera.'

He sighed and tousled the top of her hair. 'Look, you'll be fine. I'll cook you another great breakfast to get you pumped up and buzzing.'

She remembered the indigestion from the previous week. Not wanting to dampen his spirits, she smiled and shook her head. 'Thanks, but a nice poached egg on toast will be lovely.'

When Jay had left for the train and with his pep talk still ringing in her ears, she hurried upstairs to dress. She'd found what she hoped was an answer to her big bottom problem. A pair of body-shaping Spanx.

The information on the box told her the shapers would lift the cheeks of her bottom with a firming effect, and she figured she needed all the help she could get. She slid her feet into the pants, took a deep breath and pulled them firmly up her legs and thighs to her waist.

Letting her breath back out slowly she realised they were so tight she could hardly breathe. But once she'd zipped up the white knee-length skirt and turned around in front of the mirror she could see they did make a difference to the shape of her bottom. She grinned with delight. Hmm, she thought, not the most comfortable thing she had ever worn. But, as her mam would say, pride is painful. If it helped her feel better in front of the camera and David, it would be well worth the effort.

***

While she found a space in the car park Nicola remembered David's words about the semi-finals and how it was meant to test the bakers' personality, creativity and baking skills.

The main challenge, he'd told them would be to produce something altogether home-made as their signature dish which showed off their tried-and-tested recipe.

Therefore, after a whole day of deliberation she'd entered the ingredient list for her warm chocolate tart with salted caramel sauce. Not only was the tart Jay's favourite but it was a recipe she felt confident would be successful and hopefully impress David.

It was another hot day and already the sun was shining. At least we won't be making pastry again today, she thought and swung into a space to park the car.

She turned the ignition off and picked up her handbag then opened the door to climb out. However, she soon realised that she couldn't open her legs in the tight skirt and Spanx knickers. She'd slid onto the driver's seat at home, but this wasn't going to work to get out of the car. In an effort not to rip the skirt she rustled it up to her thighs and then taking a deep breath attempted a log roll action to get out of the car.

She cried out aloud as she ended up on her knees on the pavement. Oooh, she simpered, knowing she'd grazed her knees. Gripping hold of the car door to pull herself upright she saw a shadow on the pavement then a pair of black leather shoes. Her stomach lurched and she froze. She cursed under her breath that someone had found her in such a ridiculous situation. Oh, no, please don't let it be David wearing those shoes.

A voice way above her head, asked, 'Nicola, are you okay?'

She recognised Simon's voice and looked up to see his concerned face.

'Have you fallen,' he asked then placed his strong arm around her shoulders while she clambered to her feet.

She breathed a sigh of relief that it was just Simon who had passed by at the wrong moment. 'Oh, y…yes,' she stuttered. 'I just lost my footing for a second.'

She brushed her fringe from her eyes feeling like an idiot. Then realising her skirt was still up around her thighs, she cringed and hurriedly smoothed it down.

Nicola saw a smile twitch at the corner of Simon's wide mouth. He was laughing at her, she thought, but thinking about the calamity she was in, she really couldn't blame him.

She raised her eyebrows and shrugged her shoulders in a hapless manner then began to giggle, 'Well, that's a great start to the day, isn't it?'

Simon threw back his head and roared with laughter. 'Come, on, let's get inside and have a coffee.'

***

In the lady's toilets she rechecked her appearance and decided there hadn't been too much damage to her new sleek and trendy look. The darker foundation make-up she'd applied to her nose was still reflecting the light as it stated on the box, and as she looked in the mirror she smiled - there weren't any creases in her skirt. Her knees were scraped and stinging but not bleeding and they weren't visible under the skirt. She took a big sigh of relief then sprayed on more hairspray and smoothed her silky style into place. Hoping it didn't look too tacky she made her way back into the hospitality room.

***

Gratefully, she took the Styrofoam cup from Simon and sipped the coffee. 'Phew, I certainly need this after throwing myself around in the car park.'

'You'll be fine,' he reassured her. 'At least we're not on edge this week wondering what we'll have to bake. These are our own recipes, and your chocolate torte sounds great.'

She nodded. 'Yeah, it's something I usually make for family gatherings and special occasions. So, I figured it should work well?'

Simon stirred sugar into his coffee. 'It sounds lovely. I'm making a good old traditional lemon meringue pie. It's the one recipe I can make with my eyes shut because I've made it so many times before,' he said. 'Come on, let's sit down. We could be hanging around for ages yet.'

Nicola was in a quandary. She knew it made sense to sit down but she wasn't sure she'd manage to get down onto the sofa in the Spanx knickers. Also, she sighed, she wanted to look slim and sophisticated when she saw David. Her stomach churned at the thought of seeing his handsome face again and wondered what he would be wearing this week.

She smiled. 'Simon, my back is aching a little after the acrobatics, I think I 'll just stay here for now.'

He nodded and then waved as Gemma approached them.

'Hiya,' Gemma cried. 'Well, here we are again!'

She was dressed in denim shorts showing off her long-tanned legs and a pale blue, halter-neck top. Nicola sneered when she noticed Gemma wasn't wearing a bra. It was obvious that Gemma's breasts didn't require any type of assistance to stand up proudly on her chest.

Simon stared at Gemma's legs. 'Hmm,' he chortled. 'I see we're dressed for the beach today.'

A flicker of uncertainty clouded Gemma's face. 'Well, because it was so hot in the kitchen last week and as the sun is shining already, I thought I'd try to keep as cool as possible.'

She turned to Nicola and smiled. 'Do you think the shorts are too much, Nicola, I mean, is it appropriate for the TV cameras or not?'

Nicola was having trouble averting her eyes from Gemma's pointy nipples that seemed to be poking through the thin clingy material and tormenting her.

'Hey, when are shorts ever too much,' she quipped. 'But I'm sure the director will let you know if it's not quite right.'

Gemma relaxed her shoulders and grinned showing her flawless straight teeth. 'Thanks, Nicola. I knew you'd be kind enough to keep me right.'

Nicola knew the girl was desperately trying to be friendly, but she had a pain in her jaw with clenching her teeth. The muscles in her shoulders were tight in an effort to hold back the torrent of jealousy sweeping through her.

Simon shuffled his feet. 'Don't worry, Gemma, when you have your long apron on it'll cover your legs and the rest,' he said wafting his hand towards her chest.

All three swung around at the sound of David's voice as he popped his head through the door.

'Morning, all,' he called cheerfully.

Nicola watched David's eyes pop open as if they were on stalks and stare at Gemma. His whole face lit up as he strode into the room hurrying towards her. At the same time Thomas shuffled into the group behind Simon.

Gemma smiled like a princess when David took her hand and kissed the side of her cheek.

'Morning, David,' she said. 'It's another beautiful sunny day.'

While they all discussed the weather and the men eyed Gemma's legs and chest, Nicola stared down at her shoes and wanted to crawl into a hole. The impression she'd hoped to make in her pink T-shirt and plain white skirt seemed pathetic now. She wondered if there was time to nip into the toilets and remove the Spanx which she now felt were nearly cutting off her circulation.

Suddenly, the director called them through into the kitchen and they began to walk towards the door in a line behind Gemma's long legs and perfect small round bottom.

Chapter Five – Star Baker

'Have a seat on your stools first,' David instructed when they'd grouped together in the doorway. The older lady sat on one end with Thomas at the other end. Gemma, Simon and she sat in the middle.

Nicola slid up onto the stool as gracefully as she possibly could but then stared down in alarm at the small roll of flab appearing at her midriff above the waistband of her skirt. Although the Spanx was controlling the flab around her bottom it had succeeded in creating a second roll which no matter how hard she tried to breathe in would not disappear. She moaned, how hadn't she noticed this at home?

'So, here we are in the semi-finals,' David said. 'I hope you are all ready to bake your own signature dishes to show me.'

Nicola had to release the breath she was holding inside to answer along with everyone else that, yes, they were indeed ready.

Dressed today in navy-blue pleated trousers and a pale blue shirt David walked around the table. 'We'll use the same plan as last week,' he said then stopped in front of Nicola. 'And I'm dying to see what our librarian bakes for us after last week's stunning millefeuille.'

Nicola felt quite breathless and gazed into his eyes. She folded her arms across her chest hoping to conceal the roll of flab. 'Well,' she said. 'I do have a little something that is totally different to last week.'

David chortled. 'I can see that already,' he smirked and playfully flicked the side of her hair. 'I'm loving the sleek look with your hair.'

He grinned and carried along the line towards Thomas. 'And let's see if we can keep those big hands of yours a little cooler this week, eh?'

Thomas laughed good-humouredly along with everyone and Nicola smoothed her moist palms down the white skirt. He had noticed her after all, she thought dreamily, and all the extra effort had been worthwhile. She secretly hugged herself with delight at his comments and decided he probably appreciated her more subtle appearance rather than Gemma's shameless look.

While David was chatting to the director, Simon leaned towards her. 'I liked it the way it was.'

'What?' she whispered and raised her eyebrow.

He smiled. 'Your hair, I liked it the way it was.'

The director clapped his hands together loudly and instructed them to take their places at the same benches as last week.

Nicola slithered down from the stool followed by Simon and they stood waiting for the camera call to say they were ready to film. She glanced around the equipment and the small tray of ingredients checking that everything she had requested was there.

'OKAY, BAKERS,' David shouted smiling into the camera. 'Everything you need should be in front of you for your signature recipes so all that's left for me to say is, YOU HAVE TWO HOURS – NOW BAKE!'

Nicola's chocolate torte took an hour to bake on a low heat, so she immediately began to weigh out caster sugar, unsalted butter, plain flour, and pinch of sea salt. She placed the eggs carefully onto a plastic tray while collecting the tart tin, which she buttered, dusted with cocoa and then lined the bottom with baking parchment.

The director told them that David was about to walk around and talk individually and she saw him head towards Simon first with the camera. Nicola watched Simon then realised he too had spruced up his appearance from last week. The old corduroy trousers had been replaced with smart black trousers and a white shirt. His brown hair had been neatly trimmed and although David looked around five-foot-ten, Simon towered above him being at least six-foot-two.

While David discussed his lemon meringue pie, she noticed Simon looked much more confident than last week. She heard Simon agree that the shortcrust pastry he was making for the base of the pie was considerably easier than the puff pastry in the millefeuille.

As David moved on to talk to Thomas she relaxed and happily hummed a tune to herself while she prepared the remainder of the ingredients. It was different baking here than at home, but she was quickly getting used to the area, equipment, and ovens.

However, she did think longingly of her own new kitchen which had taken a large amount of the money from the divorce settlement. Its smooth lines with an eye-level double oven and a shiny red island based in the centre were worth every penny. It had been her dream kitchen that she'd always wished for and she'd laughingly told Susan that she was now happier with her kitchen than her ex-husband.

Suddenly, she looked up to see David approaching her bench followed by the camera. Remembering the tape on the floor she shuffled her feet into the correct position while opening a bar of chocolate and took a deep breath. She was determined to look good whilst being filmed.

'So, Nicola. You're making us a chocolate torte with a salted caramel sauce?' David asked. 'Can you explain to the viewers what chocolate you are using.'

'Yes,' she said smiling at him. 'I find to achieve a rich chocolate flavour it's best to use a high percentage of cocoa solids in the chocolate and the best I've ever found is this Lindt Excellence. It has 90% and is an incredibly good quality.'

David quizzed. 'Hmm, and are you ever tempted to sneak a piece while you're baking?'

She began to break the bar into pieces and drop them into a saucepan. 'Oh, no,' she giggled. 'That wouldn't be the mark of a serious baker.'

'Okay, well done,' he said and walked away towards the front of the room.

She looked across at Simon who winked at her in encouragement while she placed the saucepan over a gentle heat. Adding the sugar and butter she began to stir occasionally until it was all melted and then with a hand whisk, she stirred in the salt, flour, and eggs, one by one until the mixture was smooth. She spooned the mixture into the tart tin and placed it carefully into a roasting tin of hot water making sure the water level was one centimetre below the top. She smiled in satisfaction and slid it slowly into the oven.

It was at this stage that she realised she didn't have a timer on her bench. She noticed a timer lying on the spare bench at the front of the room and walked towards it just as David and the camera had stopped in front of Gemma.

Nicola set sixty minutes on the timer and then stood to the side making sure she was out of camera range to watch Gemma and David film. Instead of tying the long apron around her neck she noticed Gemma had only tied the apron around her waist which meant the halter neck top was visible to the viewers.

Hmm, she mused, was this done on purpose? And if so, maybe simple sweet Gemma was much cleverer than she made herself out to be in front of everyone. Or she could be hoping to find a new boyfriend when the show was broadcast by drawing attention to her obvious attributes.

While they were filming, Gemma began to talk about her strawberry cupcake recipe and how she taught it to the children at school. Vigorously, she creamed the butter and sugar together. 'I want it to be light and fluffy,' she smirked into the lens of the camera.

Nicola watched in horror as David ogled and stared at Gemma's breasts as they quivered and jiggled around with the action of the whisk. She too was captivated by the perfection and movement of them and then shook herself and frowned.

Along with the cameraman, David's eyes seemed to be transfixed and she noticed saliva collect in the corner of his mouth. She saw his Adam's apple move up and down in his throat as he swallowed hard then licked his lips.

'They're going to be absolutely delicious,' he muttered.

Nicola swore under her breath and wondered if he meant the strawberry cupcakes or her breasts.

Slowly she walked back to her bench deep in thought. If Susan were here, she would complain that this could be seen as a definite unfair advantage to the rest of the bakers. They had been told to expect a surprise judge at the final and she hoped it would be a female. Because even if she didn't make it through, it would at least give the other bakers a fairer chance against Gemma's sumptuous chest and legs.

The camera stopped filming and David went straight to the older woman at the front. Gently, he put an arm along her shoulder and walked her towards the door where one of the crew took over and she disappeared out of the room. David explained to everyone that the lady had decided to drop out of the competition because she was suffering with a migraine and felt the pressure and tension was too much for her.

Nicola nodded to herself in understanding and rubbed the back of neck. She knew how stressful it was becoming but at the same time she loved the challenge. As she reached for another saucepan, it dawned upon her just how much she really wanted to win the competition. If she had to go home at this stage and not make it through to the final, she'd feel very disappointed in herself.

David shouted, 'BAKERS, YOU HAVE ONE HOUR LEFT.'

Forcing herself to concentrate she weighed out the salt, brown sugar, whipped cream, and butter to make her caramel sauce. Nicola heard the director tell David that as they were now one contestant less, he needed to return to her bench so once again she stood on the gaffer tape on the floor.

Before he reached her with the camera, she bent down to check her chocolate torte through the glass door of the oven and smiled knowing it was baking nicely. She quickly popped back up surprising him with a big grin.

They talked through the method of making her sauce on the hob while she whisked all the ingredients together and brought it to the boil then turned down the heat to simmer before lastly adding the vanilla essence. Nicola hoped she was portraying a professional and capable impression to the viewers that would get her through to the final because it was all she could think about now. And, she thought excitedly, success would also mean being in David's company for another week.

With her chocolate torte cooling and the sauce ready she heard David call out, 'BAKERS, YOU HAVE FIFTEEN MINUTES REMAINING.'

She scattered cocoa powder on the top of the torte and placed it onto a round serving plate and then cut a triangular wedge cleanly with a sharp knife to examine the centre. She poured the sauce into a separate small glass bowl with a spoon and glanced across to Simon who was carefully placing his pie onto a serving plate.

David called, 'BAKERS, YOUR TIME IS UP PLEASE STEP AWAY FROM YOUR PUDDINGS.'

She breathed a sigh of relief before carrying the torte and sauce down to the presentation table. She'd done her very best and joined the others sitting on the line of stools. She could only pray it would be good enough for the final. It looked equally as good as Simon's lemon meringue pie and Gemma's strawberry cupcakes, but it was David's opinion that counted.

David began this time with her chocolate torte and salted caramel sauce. He lifted the wedge she'd cut and put it onto a small plate and then dolloped a spoonful of sauce onto the side. With a forkful of torte dipped in the sauce he put it into his mouth and chewed.

His shoulders sank and he moaned in delight then grinned at Nicola. 'The texture is compact and moist which is just as it should be. Although most people would serve a chocolate torte with cream, this really is quite delicious,' he said. 'The rich flavour of the dark smooth chocolate and salted caramel blend perfectly together.'

Not realising she'd been holding her breath she let it out slowly while he moved onto Thomas and his gooseberry summer pudding.

'Thomas, the gooseberries have been overcooked and are too slushy which has made the pudding wet,' David said. 'However, it has been a valiant attempt and the flavours are quite good.'

In Nicola's opinion the appearance of Simon's pie was perfect and if it tasted as good as it looked, she hoped David would give him a good review.

David said, 'The white meringue is perfectly peaked, and the lemon filling has just the right amount of lemon to suit my palate, although some people might prefer more tang. My only comment about this bake is that for the semi-final you could have been a little more creative and given it a twist with the addition of some other citrus perhaps? Or used a different theme. But it is particularly good!'

'And now our cupcake girl,' David said examining Gemma's strawberry cakes arranged perfectly on the plate.

The small paper cases were pink with white hearts and the top of each individual cake had a thick cream swirl with half a fresh strawberry in the side. Nicola had to be fair because they did look excellent but if she compared them to other cupcakes in bakery shops, she had seen more elaborate decorations. Trying to be charitable, she wondered if Gemma was aiming for a plain and minimalistic appearance.

David tasted one and raved, 'They look so inviting and the texture of the light sponge is perfect,' he said. 'And eaten with the thick smooth cream and the fresh strawberry the flavour profile is delicious!'

David signalled to the director to cut filming. 'I just need to give this some extra time before I make a decision and place them in order,' he said then went back to taste them all again.

'Okay, I'm sorted,' he said.

Nicola took a deep breath digging her fingernails into the palms of her hands praying she'd make it to the final.

David smiled. 'This is getting harder because you guys are getting better but there are only three places for the final,' he said. 'So, I will just say that I'm sorry, Thomas but you won't be going through to the final. You've done very well but, on the day, things didn't quite go your way.'

Simon was the first to commiserate with Thomas and shake his hand while Nicola squeezed his arm.

She was overjoyed with happiness and grinned at Simon who would also be taking his place in the final along with Gemma.

David interrupted them. 'And, to put the last three in order, Simon, I'm awarding third place for your pie. And although there's really very little to distinguish between the torte and cupcakes in excellent flavours, Gemma has used strawberries again which we had last week and the skill level required to make them is not as high as what is needed to make the chocolate torte,' he said. 'Which of course is entirely different to last week's bakes. So, without further ado, I'm going to award *star baker* again to Nicola.

'Oh, well done,' Simon cried and began to clap loudly.

While everyone gathered around Nicola again and while she thanked them all profusely her mind was buzzing. She couldn't ever remember feeling so alive, happy and proud of herself. To win two weeks in a row was more than she had ever dreamt possible.

Gemma gushed, 'Congratulations, Nicola. The chocolate torte and sauce look awesome!'

Nicola felt slightly embarrassed. She wasn't sure if she could have found it in herself to be so gracious if the result had been the other way around. 'Thank you, Gemma, I appreciate that.'

With filming over, David was more relaxed and invited them all to taste the bakes. Simon and Gemma went straight away to eat the chocolate torte and she tasted Simon's lemon meringue pie. Loud exclamations of, ooohs and aahs, came from everyone as they declared her torte was definitely the best bake on the table.

She glowed under their praise. 'And this pie is fabulous, Simon. It's absolutely mouth-watering. This is my mam's favourite pudding. You must give me the recipe?'

David chomped on another cupcake. 'It was a very close-run thing and I'm pleased you all agree with my decision,' he said then sighed heavily. 'But now with the heat and such a long day's filming, I'm longing for an ice-cold gin and tonic. Anyone fancy joining me?'

Simon and Thomas agreed immediately while Gemma declined claiming she had marking to do for a class next morning. Nicola was in two minds. She was desperate to get home and remove the Spanx knickers which were now cruelly digging into her waist. But when she looked into David's eyes, she knew she couldn't resist the temptation. Another hour wouldn't make that much difference if it meant spending more time in his company and especially as Gemma wasn't going to be there.

She smiled. 'I think a gin and tonic would be the prefect end to the day.'

Chapter Six – Drinks Afterwards

David insisted upon buying them all a drink at the bar and Nicola headed off to secure a table with four chairs. Music was playing in the busy pub with big groups of students celebrating and early evening shoppers. Simon and Thomas sat to her left and she placed her handbag onto the other chair to keep the seat for David.

Carrying the drinks on a tray David set them down on the table then plonked down next to her. Gratefully, they all took big gulps of the cold drinks.

'Phew, I needed that,' David said rubbing his neck. He cranked his head from side to side. 'I've been at it from six this morning.'

'It's a shame Gemma couldn't make it,' Thomas muttered.

They all nodded. And, although she'd agreed with the others, she was glad Gemma wasn't there to captivate the men with her chest and legs. She glanced sideways at David remembering the way he'd ogled Gemma. But surely that couldn't be classed as genuine interest in her, could it? Wasn't he being just like the other men and TV crew who couldn't take their eyes off such a beautiful young girl? Well, everyone except Simon who had wanted to cover her up with an apron in a fatherly manner.

While Thomas and Simon struck up a conversation David turned to face her and smiled. 'So, Ms Librarian, another win and notch on your belt.'

Her heart thumped under his direct gaze and she looked into his eyes. 'I can't quite believe it,' she said. 'And to get into the final is way beyond my dreams!'

'You deserve to be there. Your baking skills are tremendous for someone with no actual cooking qualifications. I've been amazed at all this local talent but none more than yours,' he said then lowered his voice. 'Tell me, are you this talented in other areas of your life?'

She wriggled in the chair and then felt his knee press against hers under the table. She gasped. He was flirting with her and she loved it. The bodily contact sent waves of desire shooting through her and she longed to feel the touch of his skin on hers. She teased, 'I'm not sure what you mean about other areas?'

His face was close to hers now and he whispered in her ear, 'I was thinking more of the bedroom area.'

Heat radiated across her chest and she knew her face was flushed. She felt quite light-headed with the knowledge that he seemed to want her as much as she did him. 'Let's put it this way,' she said. 'I don't think you'd be disappointed with my skills in that department either!'

'Touché,' he uttered then pulled away from her and relaxed back in the chair.

He grinned and flexed his shoulders casually linking his hands behind his head. She decided, in any other man this would look arrogant and conceited but because he was so handsome it looked like a completely natural pose. The pale blue shirt made his blue sparkling eyes even more prominent and she shivered with delight. He was so damn attractive that it was impossible to restrain her thoughts and she wished she was alone with him. She sipped the drink and daydreamed of throwing all caution aside then kissing him until he cried out for more.

Simon interrupted her thoughts by asking David where he lived.

David told them about his new apartment on the Quayside overlooking the River Tyne. 'I moved there after our separation and although I love the new property, it is only two bedroomed. But I'm looking upon it as a transitional home until I meet someone to share things with again.'

Had he glanced at her when he'd mentioned he was looking for someone? Or maybe she was just imagining it? She thought of herself rattling around alone in her big old house and how staid her life had become. The trendy apartment sounded new and exciting and she knew she'd move in with him without a moment's hesitation.

All too soon David was bidding them goodnight and stood up to leave. 'I'll see you all again next week at the final. Make sure you give your recipes a great deal of thought. It's what we call the showstopper round where we'll be looking for the most impressive creations that taste first class. It'll be the biggest test of your skill and talent, and I know the guest judge will be looking for professional standards in both appearance and flavour.'

Simon nodded. 'I don't suppose you'll tell us the name of the judge that's coming?'

'Now, Simon, you know I can't do that. It's top secret, but all I'll say is, prepare to be amazed!'

Thomas followed David out of the door and Nicola sipped her drink thoughtfully. 'Well, Simon,' she said. 'We both have to come up with something sensational.'

Simon nodded in agreement. They talked about recipes they'd tried many times before and new ones they'd read in magazines but didn't come up with anything conclusive.

Simon said, 'I suppose we shouldn't be talking like this because we are in competition with each other, but as I'm going home to an empty house, I've no one else to mull it over with.'

Nicola smiled. He was such an easy man to talk to and the one thing she loved about Simon was that he was a good listener.

'Same here, but I'll be ringing Jay when I get home, although he usually just tells me to bake all his own favourites, like the chocolate torte.'

'Well, for once he was right, Nicola, you must be enormously proud of him.'

'Oh, I am. He's doing a law degree and has worked so hard. Even though his dad left in the middle of his school exams he didn't let it affect his studies. He's definitely my blue-eyed boy,' she said and smiled. 'If he could hear me saying this, he'd cringe!'

Simon stood up to leave and Nicola drained her glass. 'I'm just going to nip into the ladies before I drive home,' she said.

He nodded, bent down, and pecked her on the cheek. 'Thanks, Nicola. I'll see you next week.'

Chapter Seven - The Final of the Northern Bake Off

At seven o'clock the following Saturday morning, Nicola was sitting calmly in the hospitality room waiting for day of the final to begin. They'd been told to be there early because the day's filming could take longer with the award ceremony scheduled for two in the afternoon.

Thankfully, it was a drizzly morning and much cooler than the previous weeks. She'd chosen to dress comfortably without the Spanx knickers in loose brown trousers and a cream blouse. However, she had bought herself a padded, plunge bra. Nicola knew she would never have the cleavage that Gemma had but leaving the top two buttons open on her blouse might just make them look more alluring.

Her stomach fluttered with butterflies when she thought of seeing David again after their conversation about bedroom skills. She was hoping to take up where they'd left off. Surely, she thought sipping her coffee, if she won the competition, he'd want to see her again and take their relationship further.

She saw Simon hurry through the door and waved. 'Morning, Simon, I've got you a coffee.'

Simon plopped down next to her and smiled his thanks. 'Lovely, I'm desperate for this today. That bloody fox has got at my chickens again through the night and I've lost two of them! I only had five to start with and they were little sweeties!'

Nicola gasped. 'Oh no, the poor little things.'

While she looked at him, dressed in black trousers and another neatly pressed white shirt which just covered his small pot belly, she smiled with affection. She realised how his face was now pleasantly familiar and marvelled at how swiftly he'd become a steady, reliable friend. She hoped they would keep in touch after the competition.

He looked down at her blouse and grinned. 'That's a nice top, you suit the colour,' he said. 'Is it new?'

She shook her head and looked into his eyes. Was he teasing her? Perhaps he'd figured out that she had designs on David. After the fiasco in the car park with the Spanx she wasn't sure what impression she had made on Simon. Hopefully, he looked on her in a friendly supportive way and didn't think her too scatter-brained.

She sipped her coffee thoughtfully and changed the subject. 'Did you stay with your decision to make the bread-and-butter pudding we talked about on the phone?'

'Yes, and thanks again for ringing me. I was in such a quandary that day,' he said smiling at her. 'And you've stayed with the lemon tart?'

She nodded. 'I had every recipe book I own out on the table that night going from one to another. But in the end, I decided that David does seem to judge mainly on taste and the Sicilian summer lemon tart seemed perfect.'

'It will be,' he said softly.

Gemma arrived and called hello from across the room. Nicola noticed a look of disappointment flash across Simon's face and wondered what had happened.

'Good, morning, finalists, gosh, I'm soooo excited,' she babbled then looked from Simon to Nicola. 'Oh, sorry, had I interrupted something?'

She noticed how Gemma was dressed more sedately this week in a blue maxi-dress with spaghetti straps and a neat white cardigan over her shoulders.

Nicola shook her head. 'No, of course, not.'

'I can't believe I've got into the final,' Gemma tittered. 'And I'm dying to know who the surprise judge is, are you?'

Simon smiled and nodded in agreement with her. 'It'll be good to have another opinion at the judging so that it's not just David's decisions all of the time.'

Nicola was mystified. 'Why,' she asked. 'Do you not think David has been accurate so far?'

The door to the kitchen opened and the director asked them to go through. Simon stood up and gently touched Nicola's shoulder as they walked towards the door. 'No, I didn't mean that. I'll just be interested to hear more comments from another professional.'

***

Sitting on the stools in front of the table Simon looked around and whispered. 'And then there were three.'

Gemma giggled. 'I know, I was just remembering the first round when there were ten of us sitting here.'

Nicola nodded, remembering how anxious she'd been and how she'd questioned her ability to even get through to the next round. 'Well, whoever wins today I think we've done fantastic just to get to this final stage,' she said.

She pushed the sleeves of her blouse up to her elbows and set her jaw ready for the challenge. She was going to give it everything she had to beat them and win.

Nicola thought the TV crew seemed louder and noisier than ever and she could tell the director was getting agitated by the way he shouted instructions and barked orders.

In a charcoal grey, slim-fitting suit and crisp white shirt David walked into the kitchen to a huge around of applause from the crew.

Nicola caught her breath. He looked absolutely gorgeous. Now she understood what Jay meant when he used the saying, simply to-die-for. His blue eyes were dancing with excitement and his smoothly shaven face was so handsome it made her swallow a lump of emotion in her throat. She felt totally overwhelmed to think that a gorgeous man like this was talking bedroom scenarios with her.

The large camera wheeled up in front of him and he pulled his shoulders back grinning suavely into the lens. 'Morning, finalists,' he said.

For one split second, she thought she heard Simon groan in a scornful manner under his breath. Surely not, she puzzled then looked out of the corner of her eye at him. It made her wonder if Simon didn't actually like David.

David continued, 'Without waiting any longer I'm going to introduce our guest judge for this show-stopping final today. And I'm sure everyone here and at home watching will want to put their hands together to welcome, Jessica Gallagher!'

Ripples of excitement ran around the room and Nicola gasped in shock and disbelief. Jessica was sixty-one, a retired celebrity cook, food writer and critic. Nicola had every cookbook she'd ever written in her kitchen and she idolised Jessica in the same way that the nation adored Mary Berry.

A small woman with short grey hair wearing a black pleated skirt and a white twinset walked briskly into the kitchen and David bent to kiss her cheek. Nicola could tell that Jessica was uncomfortable with his closeness as she pulled back sharply but then smiled sincerely into the camera and shook his hand.

With the camera rolling, David explained Jessica's achievements over the years to the viewers and ended by praising her expertise mainly with desserts and puddings.

'So, Jessica,' he said. 'Do you have anything you would like to say to the contestants before we start the competition?'

Jessica stepped forward to address them and Nicola leaned forward to listen. 'This final isn't called a show-stopper for nothing,' Jessica said firmly. 'I want to see grand, visually appealing bakes with excellent flavour profiles.'

The hairs on Nicola's arms tingled and her palms became clammy. She gulped, maybe her lemon tart wasn't creative and striking enough for the final? She cursed herself for not choosing one of her more impressive recipes. But there again, she reasoned, if they were judged on flavour alone, she knew her tart would beat anything else on the table.

She raised her eyebrows and looked at Simon for reassurance. He answered her with a wink and a big smile.

'Thank you, Jessica. I couldn't have put it better myself,' David said walking towards them. 'And as an extra bonus to the prize money and award, I'm going to take the winner as my special guest for dinner in London, to The Savoy.'

Another loud round of applause took place at his kind gesture and Nicola swallowed hard. She was gobsmacked. She pressed her hand against her chest and sucked in a deep breath. She had to win this now. Apart from the award it would be her one big chance to spend an evening with David.

She imagined walking into The Savoy linking his arm and being watched enviously by other women while she had dinner with such a strikingly good-looking man. She felt light-headed with longing and desire. And, because it was London she'd have to stay overnight in a hotel. Maybe they'd have adjoining rooms, and she could tempt him with her bedroom skills.

Hugging herself, she wondered if her little black dress would still be classed as elegant and refined. Or should she look for something more on-trend? She wanted to fit in at The Savoy and not stand out as a frumpy Northern woman with no taste or dress sense. But first, she thought through gritted teeth, she had to win this final.

Chapter Eight – Surprise Celebrity Judge

David's loud voice broke her reverie. 'OKAY, BAKERS. YOU HAVE TWO HOURS – NOW BAKE!'

Her mind was in a whirl. She'd been so lost in daydreams of David she hadn't realised they were starting, and that Gemma and Simon were heading towards their benches. Scampering after them her stomach churned with unexpected nerves.

She looked at her tray of ingredients and smoothed out the recipe sheet in front of her. Ordinarily, she didn't need to look as she knew the details so well but had already decided that following the method would help her concentrate. While she began to weigh out the butter, she saw Jessica walk towards her with the camera rolling.

Oh my God, she thought, here was her idol in the whole baking world and she was actually coming to talk to her. What would she ask, Nicola worried, and more importantly would she know the answer?

Jessica reached her bench and glanced at her name card on the bench. 'It's Nicola, isn't it?'

Nicola saw the director behind Jessica gesticulating for her to place her feet on the tape which she'd forgotten to do. She nodded her head dumbly at Jessica.

'You can keep baking while we chat,' Jessica said. 'I hear you're making us a Sicilian summer lemon tart.'

With sweaty, trembling hands Nicola lifted the bag of flour to weigh out the required amount and felt it slip onto the bench. The bag split open and fine white flour billowed out all over the bench and up into the air. She felt some settle into her fringe. Her heart was hammering, and she looked with abject horror because some of the flour had landed on Jessica's bushy eyebrows and nose.

Tears stung the back of Nicola's eyes. She'd failed at the first hurdle and disgraced herself in front of the one person she had been desperate to impress.

Following the director's actions, Jessica moved away from her bench diplomatically and mumbled that it was one of her favourite summer puddings.

When the camera whirled in another direction, Nicola saw a make-up girl hurry towards Jessica

Nicola dried her sticky hands on a tea towel and cleared the mess from her bench. Her cheeks were burning, and she was shaking. She decided to prepare the lemons while she waited for more flour to be brought. With one swift cut into a lemon, she squirted herself fully in the eye with lemon juice and yelped loudly as it stung. It was the last straw and the tears she'd been fighting back ran down her face. She wanted to run out of the kitchen and never return.

Simon had crept up next to her. 'It's okay, pet,' he said and put a finger under her chin to tilt her face upwards. With a piece of kitchen roll he wiped her cheeks.

She had never been so glad to see his familiar face and stuttered, 'I just, c-can't do it.'

'Of course, you can. It's just a small hiccup which will end up on the cutting room floor,' he soothed. 'Now, come on, forget everything else that's happened and get that tart made. You've done it hundreds of times at home. Just pretend you're in your own kitchen and crack on!'

His quiet voice and reassuring composure helped to quell her nerves and with a quivering chin she smiled at him. This whole competition wouldn't have been the same without him and she rallied herself into action.

Within minutes she'd weighed out all the dry ingredients and her hands were steady once more. She tried to follow Simon's advice and blocked out the multiple distractions from the TV crew and the stop-start rhythm of filming.

While she began to rub the fat into the flour for the pastry, she saw Jessica approach her bench again. She relaxed her shoulders, found her foot position on the floor, and determined to stay in control.

Jessica held her hands up in a submissive action as she stood in front of her smiling. 'I come in peace this time,' she chortled.

Nicola apologised profusely while she measured water into the well of her pastry mix and worked it together.

'No problem,' Jessica said kindly. 'It's all the fun of baking. And we do understand how different it can be to baking at home in peace and quiet. It took me years to get used to being filmed while I worked.'

Nicola nodded gratefully while she rolled the pastry out flat and lined her fluted-edged tin to bake blind. 'It's not often I get into a flap like that. I don't know what came over me!'

Jessica smiled. 'It's because you want to do well, which is understandable. David has been singing your praises and told me how you've been star baker at the last two sessions.'

Nicola smiled at the thought of David complementing her baking skills and felt even more determined not to let him down.

Jessica continued, 'And they tell me you're a librarian. This noisy atmosphere must be difficult for you to concentrate when you're used to total silence in the library.'

'Yes,' Nicola agreed. 'But I do love my job. Books have been one of the greatest loves of my life and I adore being surrounded by them all day. I've loved the smell of books since I was a little girl and spent hours wondering who read them before me or who would be the next person to read them. And although it is a peaceful and quiet atmosphere, we do have our moments serving the great British public.'

They laughed together and when Nicola retrieved her lemons and started to zest them proficiently, Jessica asked. 'And why are you using Sicilian lemons?'

Nicola grinned. 'Because I think they're simply the best lemons in the world. They're plump and juicy with a heady smell and the peel is fantastic for zesting. They are nothing like the hard waxed lemons from other places.'

Jessica agreed and smiled. 'I can see we think the same about using good quality ingredients in our baking.'

Nicola was enjoying the conversation, but all too soon Jessica thanked her and moved along to Simon.

While her tart was baking in the oven, she cleared the bench and watched David filming with Gemma who was making a lavender and polenta cake with violet frosting. Nicola knew it was an ambitious bake which could be fraught with obstacles, but if Gemma pulled it off, she could win the final.

So far, David hadn't spoken to any of them but was calmly walking between the three benches watching them intently. Obviously, he was leaving the conversation up to Jessica today whereas previously he had done it all.

She looked across at Simon calmly talking to Jessica. Nicola knew that if by an outside chance the judges ignored her earlier mishap, and she did win this competition it would be down to him and the way he'd calmed her down.

Simon was making white chocolate and raspberry bread and butter pudding. Wearing his glasses made him look like a business-minded accountant and she smiled at his serious expression. He was concentrating on chopping chocolate and layering bread slices into his dish.

Jessica asked him, 'I suppose you too will be used to working in a quiet office and living in your tranquil country cottage. So, all this noise and lighting while we're filming must be a distraction?'

Simon removed his glasses and looked at Jessica. 'Yes, a little,' he answered politely. 'The first week was the worst and I got into a bit of a state, but I think I've grown more confident now and like the others we've learnt to try and block it all out and concentrate on our baking.'

What a lovely response, Nicola thought then noticed David had left Gemma and was approaching her bench.

He stood with his feet planted firmly apart and his arms folded watching her closely while she heated cream and lemon juice to make the lemon custard filling. He didn't speak one word to her, and she avoided his eyes concentrating upon the task in hand.

She could, however, smell his aftershave and allowed herself the luxury of a quick daydream where she would lean across the bench and kiss him fully on the lips. Smiling to herself, she decided it might even be worth losing the competition just to feel the firmness of his lips under hers.

She peered up at him as he turned to move away and was convinced, she saw a flicker of a smile play around those lips. Her heart skipped a beat and she breathed out slowly.

'BAKERS, YOU HAVE ONE HOUR LEFT,' David shouted before moving along to Simon.

Nicola poured her filling into the pastry tart case and with a small prayer slid it carefully into the warm oven. She wanted it to be perfect to show Jessica that she could bake well without throwing flour around the room at everyone. And she had to admit, she was more in awe of Jessica than David. Jessica's good opinion would mean everything to her. She looked across at Simon who was grinning. He gave her the thumbs up signal which she took to mean he was happy with his bake.

Jessica was now in front of Gemma admiring her baked cake cooling on a rack. Gemma looked cool and calm. She hasn't even broken into a sweat, Nicola thought pouting her bottom lip. Her bake looked perfect and there wasn't a hair out of place in her long plait and clean white apron. Nicola tutted, and wondered what it felt like to excel at everything in life and be beautiful at the same time.

Jessica asked Gemma, 'You must be our young food technology teacher who David tells me is very conscientious?'

Nicola noticed Gemma give Jessica her sweetest smile yet. 'I do try to be,' she answered. 'I love the job, but the children can be a little challenging at times.'

Jessica nodded. 'Hmm, that's how I first started. I was a domestic science teacher back in the 1970s. You have my total respect because I know how hard it can be.'

Beginning to make the violet frosting with syrup, butter and sugar, Gemma said, 'That's true, but then I get so much satisfaction when I know they've understood what I'm trying to teach, and it makes it all worthwhile.'

Jessica thanked her and wished her the best of luck. She walked back to the front of the room and took a seat with David at the table and began to whisper then write comments on forms.

With her timer clutched safely in her hand Nicola wandered over to Simon. 'Thanks so much for helping me before, Simon,' she said and stroked his arm. 'I don't know what came over me. But if it hadn't been for you, I don't know if I would have got through it.'

He waved a dismissive hand. 'Ah, Nicola, I didn't do anything. This competition means too much to you to throw it all away in a few blundering moments.'

'Maybe it was baking in front of the famous Jessica Gallagher,' she sighed. 'I've idolised her for years and have all her cookbooks.'

He shrugged and smiled. 'So, that was what probably made you jittery, but when she came back the next time, she was nice to you.'

'Oh, yes,' she said. 'She made me feel totally relaxed and understands what it feels like to bake under stress.'

Simon's timer bleeped and as she turned back towards her bench, she heard him mumble, 'Which is more than can be said for his lordship!'

Just as Nicola's timer sounded and she carefully removed her tart from the oven, David shouted, 'BAKERS, YOU HAVE FIFTEEN MINUTES.'

Because of her late start she hoped the tart would be sufficiently cool in fifteen minutes but then reasoned that it wouldn't matter because the lemon tart was a bake that could be eaten hot or cold.

She watched Gemma covering her cake with the violet frosting and had to admit the colour looked stunning. Nicola bit her lip knowing she wasn't allowed to interfere. If she'd been able to help, she would have shown Gemma how to improve the appearance by making the frosting smoother and more even with a warmed palate knife. Instead, she shrugged her shoulders and returned to her own lemon tart. After leaving the tart to cool for as long as possible she lifted it onto a round glass serving plate.

Seconds later David called, 'YOUR TIME IS UP. STEP AWAY FROM YOUR BAKES.'

Nicola smiled. This would be the last time she'd hear those words and knew that whatever happened later she'd miss the competition. Carrying her serving plate she joined Simon and Gemma to walk down and place their bakes on the table.

Nicola wondered why the stools hadn't been placed in the usual places to listen to the comments, but David told them they were now free to wait in the hospitality room or go into town for a while before the award ceremony began.

'So, we mustn't find out what they think until this afternoon.' Simon said as they filed out through the kitchen door.

Nicola nodded. 'Hmm. I knew they wouldn't announce the winner until then, but I did think we'd be allowed to hear what they thought about the bakes.'

Chapter Nine – The Judges Decide

With the camera rolling, Jessica and David were ready to taste the bakes.

David said, 'Just before we start, Jessica. I can tell you that so far in round one, Nicola was better than Gemma, but last week they were practically neck and neck. And up until today Simon has never quite had the edge the other two have.'

Jessica drew her eyebrows together and nodded while David cut a triangular section from the Sicilian summer lemon tart and put it onto a small plate offering it to her first.

They both tasted the tart and Jessica relaxed her shoulders moaning softly. She looked into the camera. 'That is absolutely delicious, the flavour is sublime. And for the viewers, the words I'm going to use are tinglingly citrusy. It is also perfect in appearance, the texture of the pastry is impeccable, as is the lemon custard. I simply cannot find fault with it.'

David nodded. 'Yes,' he said. 'But Nicola did make a chocolate torte using pastry and filling last week. I would have liked her to show us a recipe using a different set of skills for the final. Although I have to agree it is simply perfection.'

David picked up a knife to cut Gemma's lavender polenta cake, but Jessica placed her hand on his arm. 'Let's look at the appearance before you cut into it,' she said. 'I think the outer covering of violet frosting could have been applied a little neater. Unless she was running out of time, I would have liked her to take a little more care with the appearance.'

He laughed loudly and grinned into the camera. 'Nooo, it looks fine to me.'

He cut a large slice from the cake and handed a fork to Jessica.

They both tasted the cake and Jessica closed her eyes while she rolled the cake around her mouth then swallowed. 'In my opinion the flavour profile wouldn't meet everyone's palate, and for me the lavender is overpoweringly sweet.'

'Never!' David argued. 'The level of flavour is perfect. The texture is light, and the concept is creative and bang on trend. And I think it's incredibly special.'

He gazed into the camera lens and gently teased Jessica. 'You're just an old-fashioned fuddy-duddy.'

Jessica drew her eyebrows together in consternation while David placed Simon's bread and butter pudding in front of them.

Swallowing a mouthful of the pudding, David said, 'My one criticism with this bake is that Simon has used shop-bought bread which is not what the competition is all about. In my opinion he should have at least baked his own bread at home to make it look more rustic.'

Jessica folded her arms under her large bust and challenged him. 'And was that explained to the contestants before the competition?'

David blushed and cleared his throat. 'I...I'm sure it was, Jessica,' he said then pulled his shoulders back. 'And in my opinion, although the bread-and-butter pudding does have a good chocolate flavour it's not special enough for the final.'

'Hmm,' Jessica muttered. 'I think the bread-and-butter pudding looks delightful and is a traditional bake with a modern twist by using the white chocolate and raspberries. There may be a few too many raspberries but they blend exceptionally well with the white chocolate.'

She stared purposefully at David. 'This is my order of results for the bakes. The Sicilian lemon tart is the best all-round bake on the table. And a draw for second place between the lavender cake and the bread-and-butter pudding. If I were absolutely pushed to split them, I would give second place to the bread-and-butter pudding and third for the lavender.'

'NO,' David shouted in alarm. 'That's not right at all!'

Jessica leaned towards him and pursed her thin lips. 'If you're not going to take any notice of my opinion why on earth did you ask me to come along and judge?'

'CUT,' yelled the director. 'We can't have this arguing in front of the viewers. We'll have to scrap that last bit.'

David shook his head slowly and stroked his chin. He apologised to Jessica whose face was flushed and pinched.

'Look,' he offered. 'Let's go back to the beginning and taste them all again and try to find a compromise.

Jessica nodded her head in agreement.

***

While Simon and Gemma collapsed spent onto the settee in the hospitality room Nicola escaped into the toilet. She gasped in horror as she looked in the mirror. Under her eyes was black smudged mascara.

The foundation on her nose had collected into a moist blob with bits of flour. And her hair looked completely bedraggled. She groaned and opened her handbag to do a quick repair with her make-up bag. The thought that David had seen her looking such a mess when he looked his absolute best, made her cringe.

Chapter Ten - The Results of the Northern Bake Off

Shortly before two o'clock, Gemma, Simon and herself were ushered by one of the crew into the large ceremony hall attached to the university. The walls in the old building were panelled in dark oak wood and rows of red velour chairs were placed in front of the small stage. The director led them up onto the stage where they were joined by the other original ten contestants who greeted them warmly.

They had been issued with two guest invitations for the ceremony and she quickly spotted Jay and Susan sitting in the front row. She smiled to see some colleagues from the library further back in the hall. Simon pointed out his sister to Nicola who gave them all a cheery wave.

While Nicola chatted with Thomas, she saw Simon talking to Gemma who pointed out a group of her pupils from school sitting behind Simon's sister.

Simon said to Gemma, 'I'd have thought to see your parents here from Leeds?'

Gemma's shoulders curled over her chest and she stared down at the floor. 'Nooo, they wouldn't do that. It would mean they'd have to stay off alcohol and drugs for the day,' she muttered. 'And that would be too much to ask of them. I've been in and out of care homes most of my childhood while they spent every penny of benefit on their addictions.'

'Good heavens!' Simon exclaimed.

Gemma mumbled, 'S...sorry, I shouldn't have blurted all that out. It's just when I saw your loved ones here to support you it made me feel bitter,' she said then lifted her shoulders and gave a little shudder. 'I don't usually think of them at all now and have put the past well and truly behind me.'

Awkwardly, Simon patted her shoulder. 'Well done. At least the children are rooting for you. You're obviously their favourite teacher.'

David strode onto the stage smiling and waving at the audience. The packed room full of people began to clap and the director and crewmen stood to the side of the stage while the camera was rolling.

'Good afternoon, everyone,' he called out cheerfully. 'Thank you all for coming along to the award ceremony for our very first Northern Bake-Off competition. And I do hope you'll all be watching on TV when it's shown next month.'

Nicola looked at the back of David as he walked in front of them and decided there wasn't one angle where he didn't look good. He introduced the other ten contestants and made funny remarks about their attempts at puff pastry. Thomas held up his large hands to which the audience laughed loudly. He told everyone how he'd been amazed at the high standards of baking in the competition and the director gesticulated at the audience to give the contestants another round of applause.

'Now, I'd like to introduce our guest judge in the competition,' he said. 'Ladies and gentlemen, it's Jessica Gallagher!'

Jessica walked onto the stage smiling and carrying a large silver award while the whole audience clapped and cheered loudly. Placing the award onto a small table she stood next to David.

Jessica smiled. 'It's been great to be in the North East and I've really enjoyed judging the first ever bake-off competition. I'd just like to read out some of the comments we've made about the three finalists because it's been such a strong competition,' she said. 'David and I have been overwhelmed with such excellent bakes which has made judging a difficult decision.'

The director gestured at the audience once more to give the contestants another round of applause.

Jessica smiled at all three finalists. 'Simon, your white chocolate and raspberry bread and butter pudding was a new twist on a traditional pudding which was very impressive.'

Simon's face flushed bright red when his sister raised her hands above her head and clapped loudly.

When the noise subsided, Jessica continued, 'Gemma, David thought the lavender cake with violet frosting was creative and bang-on trend.'

The school children in the audience cheered and whistled while Gemma grinned back at them and waved.

'And, Nicola,' Jessica said. 'I thought the flavour in your Sicilian lemon tart was absolutely sublime.'

Another huge round of applause made Nicola's legs tremble. She remembered how euphoric she had felt when she'd won star baker. She clasped her hands together tightly in her lap and hoped they would choose her. It would be even more special with Jay and Susan watching.

With a dramatic flourish David gestured into the camera. 'And now everyone, we will reveal the winner of the competition.'

The camera swung between Simon, Gemma, and Nicola. She held her breath. Her heart was hammering, and she closed her eyes then prayed, please let it be me, please say my name, David. I want the award and the dinner date with you so much.

'And the winner is…' he said.

Count-down music blared from the loudspeakers while everyone stared at him in silence. A buzz of excitement filled the whole room and the audience all sat forward in their seats gripped in anticipation.

Nicola couldn't hold her breath any longer, oh please, she begged, just say my name.

'It's, GEMMA!'

The whole of Nicola's body felt heavy and seemed to crumble inside. Bitter disappointment flooded through her and she looked wildly at Simon who was standing up with his mouth wide open in shock.

Nicola bit down hard on her bottom lip to stop tears filling her eyes. It was over and she had lost the competition.

Simon slowly shook his head and rubbed his jaw while David and Jessica approached Gemma to congratulate her. Everyone in the room began to clap loudly with the schoolchildren chanting her name.

Chapter Eleven - The Winner and Loser of the Northern Bake Off

Gemma gushed, 'I can't believe it, I'm totally speechless!'

'It's fully deserved,' David replied. 'You've been consistently good in every round and obviously saved your show-stopping lavender cake for the final which was the best bake today.'

'Congratulations, my dear,' Jessica said and handed the silver award to Gemma.

She took the award carefully in her hands and beamed at the children in the audience while they whooped and chanted her name.

Two local press photographers asked her to step to the front of the stage and hold the award high above her head, which she did with a huge grin on her face. Then she was ushered down from the stage into the audience for more photographs with the schoolchildren around her.

All of the contestants had been asked to form a semicircle in front of David and Jessica and Nicola was standing in between Thomas and Simon.

'That's going to make headlines in the newspapers tomorrow morning,' Simon whispered in Nicola's ear. 'I can just see it now - local schoolteacher bakes the best cake!'

I suppose so,' she muttered.

She swallowed back tears and squinted at Gemma wishing with all her heart it could have been her. Not only did Gemma have the award but she had a night at The Savoy to look forward to with David.

David was smiling at them all now and told them once more how amazingly well they'd all done. He handed Simon a scroll and envelope for third prize and shook his hand.

Next, he stood in front of Nicola and laid a hand on her shoulder. 'And we've awarded second prize to our local librarian for her delicious lemon tart. Sorry, Nicola, but Gemma just pipped you to the post this time,' he said softly.

She clenched her fists behind her back wanting to scream and shout at him, why, oh why, did you choose her? Was it because of the mishap with the flour or was her cake really so much better than my tart? But, with everyone clapping while Jessica handed her a scroll and envelope, she knew there was no alternative but to accept it gratefully, swallow her pride and give everyone a big smile.

***

When they joined the audience at the back of the room for a glass of wine, Susan and Jay hugged her then Simon introduced his sister.

'Oh, Mam, you aren't too disappointed, are you,' Jay asked with a worried frown. 'I mean, second prize is still a great result.'

'Nooo,' she exclaimed sneaking her arm around his waist. 'Of course, I'm not. I'm more than delighted to have been made runner-up.'

Susan nodded and clinked her glass on the side of Nicola's. 'And you have been star baker for two weeks running. So, I would say, if what David said about the high level of professional baking is true, you both did great just to get in the final.'

Nicola looked at Simon and smiled. 'Susan's right, we both did really good!'

Simon nodded. 'Hmm, I know but I'd have loved to have been a fly on the wall when they were tasting the bakes,' he said and cocked his head. 'I simply cannot believe that lavender cake was better than your tart.'

Nicola smiled gratefully and laid a hand on his arm. 'Thanks, but I probably lost a few marks after my incident with the flour,' she said.

Nicola told them all how she had managed to coat Jessica's eyebrows with flour.

Jay hooted, 'Way to go, Mam.'

Susan giggled, and Simon's sister threw her head back and roared with laughter.

Jessica approached the group quietly from behind. 'Well,' she said. 'Everyone seems to be enjoying themselves in this corner.'

Nicola swung around to greet her and introduced everyone. 'I was just telling them about the flour,' she said. 'And once again, I must apologise to you, Jessica.'

Jessica waved a dismissive hand. 'No need. I just wanted to catch you before I left for my train,' she said and pointed to a small overnight case propped against the wall. 'I'd like you to know that I thought your lemon tart was truly amazing, and in my opinion should have won on the taste alone, which was divine.'

Jay's face was beaming, and Susan had watery eyes. Nicola could feel her cheeks flush as she thanked Jessica. To have this praise from her idol was a heady experience. She wanted to squeal and jump up and down with happiness. But did it make up for not winning and having dinner with David?

Jessica bid them all farewell then turned to leave. Quietly she leaned towards Nicola's ear and whispered, 'And I do think dinner at The Savoy will be very overrated.'

Simon took Jessica's arm and carried her case down the stairs and outside to the taxi rank.

Most of the audience had dwindled away and her friends had gone back to the library. Susan took her hand, and they made their way in search of the lady's toilets.

***

Jessica's comment whirled around in her mind. Did she mean the food at The Savoy was exaggerated? Or perhaps she meant David's company would be overrated? When they left the Ladies, she heard the familiar voices of David and Gemma in the corridor. Grabbing Susan by the arm she pulled them both back behind the wood-panelled door so they would be out of sight but could still hear their conversation.

Gemma was standing with her back against the wall. David stood in front of her with a hand outstretched on the wall above her head. 'That lavender cake was so special that I had to give you first prize and it was very exotic, just like you are,' he uttered. 'You're such a babe magnet that I can't wait to take you to The Savoy to congratulate you properly!'

Nicola's heart was hammering loudly in her chest and she could feel Susan's arm shivering with excitement in the conspiracy. Nicola poked her head around the door just in time to see Gemma duck out from under David's arm and slither along the corridor. 'The dinner isn't really necessary,' she told him.

Nicola was furious and dug her nails into the palms of her hands. She wasn't sure whether she hated David as much as Gemma, or vice versa. Holding Susan's arm, she lifted her chin and marched them both out into the corridor and along to the ceremony hall. Vaguely, in the distance she heard David calling her name but didn't stop until they got back inside the hall.

***

'The bloody cheek of him!' Susan exclaimed loudly. 'What's his game? Coming on to you for weeks then because you don't win, he's crawling after the young girl?'

And why didn't I win, she thought listening to Susan rant.

Jessica had already said she would have given me first prize, therefore it had to be David who thought Gemma's cake was the best. She couldn't ever remember feeling so disappointed in herself. She'd lost the fight and young Gemma had waltzed off with the award and the dinner-date.

Nicola nodded and agreed with everything Susan said then plastered the false smile back onto her face. She swallowed hard trying to hold back her tears. All she wanted now was to go home and lick her wounds.

***

Back in the hall, Jay left to join his friends and Susan bid her farewell just as Simon reappeared.

'Come and have a drink with me?' he asked. 'I've been chatting to Jessica in the taxi queue and have news to tell you.'

'Oh, Simon, I'm bushed,' she said but saw his shoulders slump and relented. 'Okay then, just a quick one.'

They left the hall together and went down the grand staircase and out onto the pavement. Suddenly, at the sound of heels on the wooden stairs they both turned to see Gemma running past them and outside towards a young guy.

Nicola thought he looked like a Greek god as Gemma kissed him full on the lips, jumped into his Mazda and they sped away from the roadside.

'Ha!' she snorted and raised her eyebrows at Simon. 'David isn't going to get anywhere with her at The Savoy. After all the flirting he's done, she actually has a boyfriend!'

Simon sighed heavily. 'Come on, let's get that gin and tonic. I think we deserve it.'

***

While Simon stood at the bar in the same pub they had been in last week, Nicola sighed and gazed across at the table where she'd sat next to David. She remembered how he'd flirted with her and rubbed his leg against hers. She frowned, how could she have misread those actions and got it so wrong?

Simon joined her and handed her a tall glass of gin and tonic. They both took big gulps.

'Ah, that's better,' Simon said.

Nicola nodded and felt her shoulders relax. 'You're right there, Simon. I could have done with this when I chucked flour at Jessica!'

He laughed. 'Anyway, I just wanted to tell you what Jessica told me,' he said. 'And although she didn't actually say the words, apparently there was quite a bit of arguing and disagreement between her and David about the prizes.'

Nicola leaned towards him and felt her pulse quicken. 'Go on,' she said.

Simon paused, 'Seemingly Jessica wanted to give your tart first prize, and then me and Gemma drawn second. And, if she'd really been pushed to choose, she would have given my pudding second place above the lavender cake because she thought Gemma's flavour profile was too sweet.'

Nicola digested this information and grinned. 'Really?'

He nodded and then smiled with flushed cheeks. 'I can't believe she actually liked my pudding that much!'

Nicola thought he looked like a little boy receiving a good exam mark at school. 'Well, I can,' she stated and smiled. 'At last, you've received some recognition for your great bakes.'

It began to dawn upon her what had actually taken place and she knew she'd have to ask the question. She took a deep breath. 'So that means David definitely overruled Jessica's decision?'

Simon nodded gravely. 'It certainly looks that way, Nicola. And you should have won that final!'

She shrugged her shoulders. 'Oh, well, it's too late now.'

He tutted. 'Well, I think it proves that David is the moron I've thought he was from day one. And he's awarded the lavender cake first prize because he wants young Gemma on his arm at The Savoy.'

She gasped with surprise at Simon's reaction and the disgust she saw in his eyes and expression. She remembered what she'd seen in the corridor with Susan and lowered her head then told him what they'd heard.

He shook his head slowly. 'This is totally unfair,' he said. 'I suppose you could contest the decision with the programme bosses or the director?'

She frowned. 'No, I'll just let it go. I couldn't stand the aggravation.'

Imagining Gemma hanging onto David's arm in The Savoy, she puffed out her cheeks and blustered. 'B...but there's no way young Gemma will be interested in him, now that she's got herself a gorgeous hunk of a boyfriend,' she said. 'And it bloody well serves David right!'

Simon sat back in the chair folded his arms and stared at her.

She had become used to his mannerisms over the weeks and could tell he was mulling something over in his mind.

'What,' she asked and tilted her head to one side. 'What are you thinking about?'

'Well,' he said. 'I'm trying to decide whether to tell you about Gemma and what I learnt earlier in the hall.'

She leaned towards him. 'Oh, Simon, you have to now,' she said and patted the back of his hand.

For the first time she noticed there was a white band-mark on his brown fourth finger where he'd obviously removed his wedding ring.

He sipped his drink and told her about Gemma's neglectful childhood and parents. 'I think that's why she seems desperate to please everyone all of the time. The poor thing must be starved of any type of affection and was clamouring for our attention.'

Nicola pressed her hands against her flaming cheeks and felt a cold shiver flood through her. She gulped and remembered the awful thoughts she'd had about Gemma then lowered her chin to her chest.

'Oh, God, to use one of Jay's expressions, I feel crap. I haven't been very nice to her, I'm afraid,' she muttered. 'In fact, I've behaved like, well, I don't know what?'

She was flustered unable to think of a word to describe the unreasonable jealousy she'd levelled against Gemma.

Simon volunteered, 'You thought of her as a rival,' he said. 'Nicola, there's nothing wrong in being competitive.'

She smiled at him gratefully and relaxed back in her chair. Without doubt he was one of the kindest men she'd ever known. Even when she was trying to admit her failings, he was still making them sound reasonable and just.

But she knew that her treatment of Gemma had been shameful and when she thought about the girl's terrible upbringing in comparison to the way she'd spoilt her own son it made her shudder.

The only way she would feel better about this situation would be to try and make amends. 'Maybe I could get Gemma's number and ask her to my house for dinner,' she said. 'She could meet Jay and although he's younger than her, he could take her into Newcastle to the pubs and clubs where she might make more friends?'

Simon nodded. 'Good idea. But I do think David is to blame for much of this upset. I've known what type of man he was since the first time he walked into the kitchen. He's shallow and conceited enough to think that any woman would fall at his feet,' he said. 'Which for a man of his age to chase after such a young girl is nothing short of ludicrous. In fact, it's incredibly sad in a way.'

She nodded and slowly digested his words. 'Yes, you're right there,' she said.

Tears clogged in her throat. She'd been one of the women playing right into his hands. Nicola raged at herself for being crazy to think a guy as good looking as him could ever be interested in her. She cringed remembering how besotted she'd been and how she had swooned about him to Susan.

Nicola thought of her friend and knew if she were here now, she would tell her to count her blessings that she'd found out his true character before it went any further. Which she knew was right and sensible.

She gazed across the room avoiding Simon's eyes. She'd never been level-headed around good-looking men, especially her ex-husband, and once again she had been taken in by them and behaved like a fool. Susan had often told her that good looks were only superficial, and Nicola sighed, when would she ever learn her lesson?

She fiddled with a beer mat on the table. 'David is nothing but a tanned pathetic creep,' she muttered.

She couldn't bear to look up at Simon. 'And I've been a complete idiot. I thought on the first week that he was interested in me and stupidly I tried to look trendier and younger for him,' she pouted then shook her head. 'I even tortured myself trying to change the shape of my bum by wearing Spanx and a push-up bra in the hope that he'd notice me.'

She felt his finger lifting her chin and she looked up into his eyes.

He grinned at her. 'I happen to be particularly fond of your bottom. I've watched it bending over the oven for days now,' he teased. 'And that blouse is very enticing!'

She swallowed the ball of emotion gathering in her throat and giggled. The bubbles in the tonic water sprayed up under her nose and made her eyes water. She sniffed and protested. 'Oh, stop it, Simon!'

He pulled a large white handkerchief from his pocket and handed it to her. 'That's better, Nicola, I hate to see you look unhappy,' he said. 'And if you really want to go to The Savoy, I'd gladly take you because in my eyes, and Jessica Gallagher's you are the real winner of the Northern bake off.'

His genuine smile lit up his whole face and she noticed his deep brown eyes. Wow, she thought blowing her nose, why hadn't she seen them before?

Nicola felt as though she was looking at him for the first time and knew she liked what she saw. He certainly was an attractive man. Perhaps she'd been so wrapped up in David-the-creep, she hadn't noticed Simon in that certain way. She stared into his eyes and took a deep breath.

He beamed and held eye contact with her. 'Em, Nicola,' he said. 'I'm a bit out of practise with this but will you have dinner with me one night?'

She nodded then parted her lips with feelings of desire racing through her body. 'I'd love to,' she said, and hoped he was going to kiss her.

He cleared his throat. 'Oh, thank God you've agreed. I've wanted to ask since the day I picked you up off your knees in the car park.'

She stared longingly at his lips. He lowered his head to cover her lips with his mouth. Responding to his kiss she wrapped her arms around his neck and knew she had been the overall winner of the Northern Bake Off.

If you have enjoyed this story - A review on amazon.co.uk would be greatly appreciated.
You can find more from Susan Willis here:

NO CHEF, I Won't! https://amzn.to/3j1HiGn

Can kneading bread be fun with your man? And, would you refuse an invite to your handsome neighbours' greenhouse to see his wonderful courgettes? These are just two problems Katie must wrestle with in this food lovers romance. Katie's partner, Tim lands a new job as head chef in a London restaurant. He changes from the sweet-natured, food loving guy she fell for and becomes unbearably arrogant. 'Yes Chef!' respond his browbeaten assistants as he barks orders at them across a steamy kitchen. But when he treats Katie this way, she rebels and after a huge row, she walks out. With the help of her two close friends, she rebuilds her single life and starts a successful catering business. Tim realises what he's lost and wants her back, but Katie is not sure.
Will she say, 'Yes, Chef.' Or 'No, Chef, I Won't!'

Ebook Cosy Crime Short Reads:
Christmas Intruder https://amzn.to/38ZpyZj
Megan's Mistake https://amzn.to/2pl88Sf
An Author is Missing https://amzn.to/2N1DAOX

Website www.susanwillis.co.uk

Twitter @SusanWillis69
Facebook m.me/AUTHORSusanWillis
Instagram susansuspenseauthor
pinterest.co.uk/williseliz7/

Recipes from the Final of the Northern Bake Off
Follow these simple recipes by my good friend, Samuel Goldsmith to make the final three bakes, Sicilian Summer Lemon Tart, Lavender Polenta Cake with Violet Frosting, and White Chocolate and Raspberry Bread and Butter Pudding.

White Chocolate and Raspberry Bread-and-Butter Pudding
One of the ultimate combinations: white chocolate and raspberry. Combined with a bread-and-butter pudding it gives a contemporary feel to a traditional dessert.

8 slices of white bread
50g butter, softened
100g white chocolate, chopped
225g raspberries
284ml double cream
250ml full fat milk
3 eggs
1 tsp vanilla extract
2 tbsp sugar

Butter the bread on one side and cut each slice into four triangles. Lay half of the bread on the bottom of an ovenproof dish (roughly 10 x 8 inches). You will need to overlap them. Sprinkle over half of the chocolate and raspberries and cover with the remaining bread, overlapping again. Measure the cream and milk in a jug and then beat in the eggs, vanilla extract and sugar. Carefully pour over the bread and allow to soak for 20-30 minutes. Scatter over the remaining chocolate and raspberries and bake in a pre-heated oven at 180C/gas mark 4 for 20–30 minutes or until the custard is set. Serve warm.

Lavender and Polenta Cake with Violet Frosting

Perfect served with an afternoon tea; you can glam it up by slicing it in half lengthways and adding an extra layer of frosting and sprinkling over some crystallized violets, or fresh if you have them. It can also be served without the frosting for those who have less of a sweet tooth.

250g butter, softened
250g caster sugar
2 tbsp lavender
½ tsp lavender extract
1 tsp vanilla extract
3 eggs
200g, self-raising flour
100g polenta
50 ground almonds
½ tsp baking powder

Frosting

100g butter, softened
150g icing sugar
¼ – ½ tsp violet syrup

Cream the butter and sugar together until light and fluffy (this means until it is almost white and meringue like – usually takes about 10 minutes in an electric mixer). Sprinkle in the lavender and lavender and vanilla extracts.

In a medium-large bowl mix the flour, polenta, almonds and baking powder together.

Add one third of the flour mixture in with the creamed mixture and mix until combined.

Beat in one of the eggs into the butter mixture and follow with another third of the flour mixture and continue this process until the eggs and flour mixture have been used up. Mix until combined.

Pour the mixture in to an 8-inch, deep cake tin and bake in a preheated oven (180C/gas mark 4) for 40 minutes or until a knife comes out clean (this may take slightly longer, time varies even when using the same oven).

Allow cake to cool in the tin for 5 minutes before removing to a cooling rack to cool completely.

Beat together the butter, sifted icing sugar and a teaspoon of warm water. Mix in the violet syrup to taste; brands differ so it's important not to add too much all in one go. Spread the frosting over the top of the cake and serve.

Sicilian Lemon Tart

It's really important for a lemon tart to be tart, not only in the sense that it has pastry but also it should give a real zing in the mouth. Reducing the lemon juice helps to give it this zing. When you're making the pastry be sure to handle it as little as possible, you're more likely to get a better result in a food processor because there is less heat being given off which should result in a shorter texture.

Pastry

75g butter, cold
125g plain flour
1 egg yolk

40g caster sugar

1 lemon, zested and juiced (keep the juice for the filling)

Filling

4 eggs

2 egg yolks

6 lemons, all juiced and 3 zested

300ml double cream

250g caster sugar

First of all, make the pastry. Rub the butter in to the flour until you reach a breadcrumb like texture then mix in the caster sugar and lemon zest. Make a well, add the yolk in to the centre and mix it through. It is unlikely that this will be enough to combine the mixture into a dough so add a little cold water (½ tsp at a time, you should need no more than a couple of teaspoons) until the dough has combined – you can, of course, do all this in a food processor. Refrigerate for 10 minutes. Roll out on a lightly floured surface until it is big enough to line a 20cm tart tin. Line the tin (don't worry if it's a little crumbly when you roll it out just patch it together in the tin), make a few holes in the base with a fork and place back in the fridge for 10 minutes. Pre-heat the oven to 180C/160C (fan)/gas mark 4, remove pastry case from the fridge and line with greaseproof paper and baking beans (or a suitable alternative) and bake for 10 minutes. Remove the baking beans and foil and bake for a further 7 minutes. The pastry should be a biscuit-like colour and cooked through, if it's not, place back in for a few more minutes.

Filling time. Juice the lemons (zest 3 of them first otherwise you'll find it tricky later) and add to the juice kept over from the pastry. Reduce the juice by a third (you should end up with around 175ml juice) by boiling over a high heat. Leave to cool. Whisk the eggs, yolks, cream and caster sugar together until combined and then mix in the cooled lemon juice, pass through a sieve if you think it looks lumpy, and then mix in the lemon zest. Place the custard mix into a saucepan and heat over a low to medium heat, stirring continuously until you have reached a lemon curd like consistency. Pour into the ready-made pastry case. If you're feeling confident you can sprinkle over a couple of tablespoons of sugar and grill/blow torch the tart to give a caramelised topping.